TRAIL OF SHADOWS

Center Point
Large Print

Also by Lauran Paine and available from
Center Point Large Print:

Ute Peak Country
Way of the Outlaw
The Plains of Laramie
Guns in Wyoming
Man from Durango
Prairie Empire
Sheriff of Hangtown
Rough Justice
Gunman's Moon
Wyoming Trails
Kansas Kid

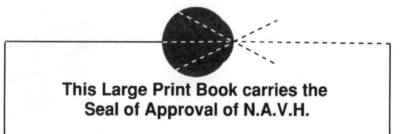

**This Large Print Book carries the
Seal of Approval of N.A.V.H.**

TRAIL OF SHADOWS

A Western Story

LAURAN PAINE

CENTER POINT LARGE PRINT
THORNDIKE, MAINE

This Circle Ⓥ Western is published by
Center Point Large Print in 2015 in co-operation with
Golden West Literary Agency.

First Edition
June, 2015

The text of this Large Print edition is unabridged.
In other aspects, this book may vary
from the original edition.
Printed in the United States of America
on permanent paper.
Set in 16-point Times New Roman type.

ISBN: 978-1-62899-595-4 (hardcover)
ISBN: 978-1-62899-600-5 (paperback)

Library of Congress Cataloging-in-Publication Data

Paine, Lauran.
  Trail of shadows : a western story / Lauran Paine. — First edition.
  pages cm
  Summary: "Todd Duncan barely escapes a lynch mob who believes he
murdered the express agent in town. The only way to convince them
that he's innocent is to track down the real killer"
  —Provided by publisher.
  ISBN 978-1-62899-595-4 (hardcover : alk. paper)
  ISBN 978-1-62899-600-5 (pbk. : alk. paper)
  1. Large type books. I. Title.
  PS3566.A34T727 2015
  813′.54—dc23

                                                    2015010053

CHAPTER ONE

Where the sun struck down upon open country out beyond the pines there lay a broad belt of green, but beyond that where the land turned gray and inhospitable was pure desert. The river made that green belt. It ran from east to west. For a full mile on either side was greenery and good foliage where underground seepage fed searching roots.

It was a land of hard contrasts. Northward, where the forested slopes stair-stepped their way up and over those squatting hills, lay a fragrance and a coolness. Southward, beyond that belt of green, were bitter earth and stark stone buttes, dry riverbeds, and gravelly soil that put up clouds of alkali dust to burn a man's eyes and sting his throat.

There was a town down there, easterly in the heartland of that green country. From halfway up a tilted hillside Duncan saw it, caught the bitter reflection of sunlight off roof tops and windows, and looked long in that direction because this was the first town he'd come across in nine days of traveling.

The pull of that town was strong, and yet Duncan went on around it, southward. He halted once in a fringe of trees to the west to rest his horse, smoke, and assess that onward desert, then he continued on his way as men do who have some purpose in mind. He passed on out of the greenery and down into that other world of grayness and sun scorch and graceful desert paloverdes.

He rode all day and near evening, with seven miles behind him, sighted two tall cottonwood trees a little to the east, and about a mile southward. He made for those trees. Cottonwoods on the desert meant water, and while seasoned travelers frequently made their nighttime dry camps, they never did this from preference.

Daytime's final red ribbons of sunlight lay crimson over the land giving the desert an eerie complexion, as though in all this brooding silence there was nothing but bitterness and sadness. This mood went into Duncan, leaving him restless and anxious to get on across this place, but his spirits lifted a little when, nearing those two cottonwoods, he spied a grazing horse with sweaty saddle stains upon his back. Company would be welcome to Duncan. His spirits lifted a little as he speculated on what kind of a range man he would find up ahead.

There was a little minute oasis around those cottonwoods with a still water pond in the center of it. It was not yet full summer so that pond did not as yet have the greenish scum around its edges it would acquire later on, when the heat of day and the heat of night kept water temperatures lukewarm twenty-four hours. For a while yet, then, it would be safe for men and animals to drink here.

Duncan did not consider the roundabout country as he neared the trees, the tough grass, and the cottonwoods. He was instead concentrating upon locating the man who was camped there, the man who owned that grazing bay horse.

He saw him, finally, when he came out of the last scattering of brush and into the spongy area around the spring. He was near there across the little meadow with his shoulders to one of those cottonwoods, with his head slumped, asleep.

Duncan was weary himself. He understood how a man could drop off before he'd even built his little fire and had his supper. The stranger's saddle was over there beside him. His carbine was leaning upon the same tree and the man's six-gun had been drawn forth and placed close at hand upon the saddle.

Duncan swung down, turned to offsaddling, and told himself that there was nothing at all wrong with being wary in a strange country. He would get a cooking fire going, cook a pot of coffee, then awaken the strange cowboy.

He did this, made his twig fire, set the coffee to boil, put on a skillet of side meat to fry, made himself a smoke, and sat there across the pond from the sleeping stranger, feeling comfortable in the dying day. His fire merrily danced, lancing at the oncoming dark with its whipping red blades. The aroma of coffee and meat cooking made Duncan acutely aware of his day-long fast. He sat there, cross-legged, turning drowsy and relaxed and pensive. Regardless of a man's situation, whether riding into an unknown desert or crawling up a hill under the searching slash of gunfire, at day's end this quiet time with its good odors made everything else seem worthwhile.

Duncan put out his smoke, swung to see if the barely discernible stranger over there in the gloom had awakened yet, then got up to cross over because the man hadn't moved.

Duncan paused to lie belly down and drink at the pool. Afterward he continued on around to where the other man was, halted in front of him, and wagged his head. This one sure slept. He doubted very much if anyone could walk up on him like this in his sleep. He kneeled, said— "Hey, fellow, the coffee's hot,"—and when there was no response, he put forth a hand and gently shook the stranger's shoulder. The cowboy slumped lower, his head rolled aimlessly as he gradually eased over sideways and very slowly, very relaxedly fell over upon his side. His hat dropped off and rolled away. Duncan was looking into a pair of wide-open glazed eyes.

The shock kept Duncan from moving for nearly thirty seconds. This man was dead, had been dead right from the start when Duncan first saw him over here. Now several other things Duncan had earlier rationalized about came back to jar him with a different, a sinister import. That carbine leaning against the tree. That six-gun lying there within a foot of the dead man's right hand. That saddle turned up onto its side like that—a man could drop down behind that in a second. And finally, the sweat stains on the tucked-up horse. This man had been riding hard when he came upon the cottonwood spring.

Duncan rocked back on his heels. He blew out a big breath. He eased down onto one knee and pushed forth a hand to gently lift the dead man's Levi jacket. Even with so little light to see by there was no mistaking that sodden place near the center of the dead man's chest. He had been shot. Duncan dropped the jacket, drew back his arm, and leaned there totally absorbed in this eerie mystery. He had no idea he was not alone until a voice called over to him, sounding cold and deadly.

"Stay like you are, fellow! Make one move and you're dead."

Duncan's shoulders bunched at the suddenness of this voice, and yet his absorption in the mystery in front of him was so complete it took him a moment more to understand that he was under someone's gun. He did not move. Behind him he heard men moving, muttering back and forth, then one of those men began pacing around the pool. Duncan listened to those soft footfalls, knew exactly when the stranger was behind him, and a second later felt his hip holster go light.

"Stand up," ordered his captor. Duncan stood. "Turn around."

Duncan turned. He was looking into the gray whisker-stubbled face of a short, heavily-muscled man with a small but quite distinct half-moon scar high on his left cheek, and with deep-set uncompromising blue eyes as clear and as cold as ice. Over this man's shoulder Duncan saw the others on across the pond where Duncan's fire was. There were three of them, all as travel-stained as the one in front of him, all as watchful and heavily armed.

"Well, he made it, didn't he?" said the short man, holding Duncan's own gun cocked and ready in his right fist. "We had bets amongst us that he'd never get to you . . . not with that slug through his lights from back to front."

The short man motioned Duncan aside with the cocked gun, stepped up, flopped the dead man over with his boot toe, bent for a long, close look, then straightened around motioning for Duncan to precede him back around to the little cooking fire.

"I never underestimated him," he growled at Duncan as they started away from the dead man, "but I got to hand it to him . . . he was tougher even than I thought he was."

Duncan got over to his fire. He looked at the others; they were eating his side meat and drinking his coffee. They grinned at him as though amused at something, as though tickled that they should be eating the food he'd prepared.

Each of these three men was tall. One was thick-shouldered and heavy but the others were typical, lank, leaned-down range riders, tough as an old boot. The short one with the crescent-shaped scar on his left cheek seemed to be the leader. He eased off the hammer of Duncan's gun, pushed the weapon into his waistband, and accepted a tin cup that he began to sip.

That was when Duncan finally spoke. "Mind if I have a little of my own coffee?" he dryly asked.

"Sure not," said one of the grinning men, who stooped, caught up a full cup, and presented it to Duncan.

All three of the tall men stood there eyeing Duncan, still grinning. The short man did not smile, although he too kept his unwavering glance upon Duncan.

"A few other questions. Just who the hell are you fellows? Who the hell is that dead man over there? And what the hell do you think you're doing . . . taking my gun?"

One of the lank men put a raffish gaze upon Duncan. "The preacher'd be plumb sorrowed to hear you cuss so much," this man said. "You ought to think of him, y'know. Must be rough on the old fellow havin' a boy like you."

Duncan's brows rolled together. He considered each of those four men over an interval of silence, fixed the shorter, thicker of these strangers with his gaze and wagged his head.

"I can tell you one thing, boys. I don't know what you're talking about, but if you figure I'm tied up some way with that dead fellow over there . . . you're about as wrong as mortal men can get."

The heavy-set tall man finished his coffee, flung away the dregs, and tossed down his cup near the fire. He was gray over the ears and grizzled in the face. He let his ironic smile atrophy as he solemnly said: "If I've heard that once before, I've heard it a hundred times. Tell me, Parton, why don't you fellows ever think up something original?"

Duncan sipped his coffee, trading stares with this older man. When he finished with the coffee, he said: "You think my name is Parton . . . is that it?"

The big man sighed resignedly. "Yup."

Duncan fished in a pocket, brought forth two letters, and handed them to the big man. "See the name there . . . Todd Duncan."

Those four men crowded up and looked down. The first one to speak was a youngish man, and this one was still half grinning, but his eyes behind the half droop of lids were deadly. This one would kill at the drop of a hat.

"Who'd you rob on the way down here?"

Duncan assessed this youngest of the four, saw him for precisely what he was, and did not answer him.

The short man stepped away. "You got anything else with that Duncan name on it?" he asked.

"Aw hell, Matt," laughed the youngest man. "Don't tell me he's takin' you in with those letters? Why, hell . . . we followed that other one down here straight as an arrow. We stood out there in the brush watchin' this one make supper for the pair of 'em . . . even lay out two cups and two plates . . . then go over and see if he could help that one I shot. I say string him up to one of those cottonwoods."

The short man called Matt let all this go by without interruption, then he repeated his earlier question to Duncan and stood there waiting.

Duncan had nothing else with which to identify himself. In fact it was only by accident that he'd kept those letters. They were from an old friend of his up in Cheyenne, a rider he'd worked with in the north country. He just hadn't gotten around to throwing them away yet.

"No," he said. "That's all I have."

"String him up," the youngest of his captors growled again. "Never mind all this damned talk."

CHAPTER TWO

"You're too dog-goned quick with your mouth," the scar-faced, short man growled at the youngest of those four. "Have another cup of coffee and shut up."

Duncan thought he sensed indecision in the scar-faced man. "Mind telling me what this is all about?" he asked mildly.

"Don't mind at all," answered up the heaviest of those three tall ones, gazing steadily over into Duncan's eyes. "That's your friend Jerry Swindin over there. Right after the pair of you tried robbin' the express office up in Leesville he got shot. He got this far before he died. We figured the pair of you split up to throw us off your trail. Well, it worked until we figured if we stayed after Swindin he'd eventually lead us to you. And he did."

"I guess," said Duncan, "if I told you I've never been in this place you call Leesville in my whole cussed life, you wouldn't believe me, would you?"

The big man shook his head. In the same even tone he said: "No, mister, I wouldn't believe you. And maybe, except for the killin' of Charley Dudley, I wouldn't give a damn either. But you see, old Charley was a good friend of mine."

"Who was Charley Dudley?"

"The express clerk, mister. I don't know whether you or Swindin killed him, but I aim to find out, for, like I said . . . Charley was a good friend of mine. We grew up together."

"I see," Duncan murmured, catching the youngest man steadily staring at him from farther back. He added: "One more question . . . who is the preacher your friend back there spoke of?"

"He's your paw. Now, if you're through actin' stupid, suppose we start back."

"Back," snarled the youngest man. "Jack, I say string him up right here. There ain't another decent tree for the job until we get plumb back to town."

Two of the others, although they did not openly agree with this suggestion, looked at Duncan as though they certainly would lend a hand at yanking on the rope. Neither the scar-faced man nor the big, burly, older man who was standing in front of Duncan looked willing to lynch him or let others do it. He decided he'd be wise to make some kind of overture to these two.

"Listen," he said to the big, powerful man across from him. "My paw's no preacher, my name is Todd Duncan, not something-or-other Parton. I never saw that dead man over there before in my life, and I've never been in your town."

The scar-faced man spoke from over by the little

fire where he was squatting. "You'll get a chance to see our town, Parton. You'll get a chance to be identified by that dog-goned Bible-banger, too. You see, he didn't get away. We got him locked up in my jailhouse."

Duncan squinted. "Your jailhouse, mister?" he said.

The scar-faced man fished in a shirt pocket, brought forth a well-worn nickel badge, held it palmed so Duncan could see it before returning it to his pocket. "Sheriff Matt Berryhill," he said. "If I'd been in town when you and Swindin tried that express job, neither of you'd have gotten this far, believe me."

Something here troubled Duncan. If these men knew Swindin so well, knew this Preacher Parton, too, then how was it that they mistook him for the third member of that outlaw crew? He asked Sheriff Berryhill about this and his answer was curt.

"Cut it out, Parton. You're stalling and you're wasting time. Sure we knew Swindin. He came to town with the preacher and we saw him around the saloons. We also saw you . . . some of us anyway . . . but never up close . . . never in town, but always out at the preacher's camp at the riverbank." Sheriff Berryhill looked up, his gaze hard. "If you think that's going to save you, you're dead wrong. Circumstantial evidence says you were in on it with Swindin and the preacher, and in this country, Parton, circumstantial evidence has hung its share of men where murder's been done."

Duncan stepped around to the fire. He squatted there and reached for the coffee pot. He had a sick feeling in his guts, and yet, for some reason, he couldn't altogether absorb what was happening to him. It was too unreal, too smoothly condemning. Sure, he'd laid out two cups and two tin plates when he'd started his cooking fire, but, hell, range etiquette said you always offered folks a meal at mealtime.

Maybe it did look like he'd purposefully rendezvoused here with Swindin, but he hadn't at all. That was purest coincidence. The trouble with his reasoning, he knew, was that only he was influenced by it. All he had to do was cast one look around him at those four bitter faces, and he knew just how futile anything he might say would be.

He finished his coffee, put the cup aside, and went to work fashioning a smoke. As he lit up, blew outward, he considered that lawman sitting over there. Duncan was lucky. If this sheriff hadn't been with these men—if that youngest rider had been the influencing factor here—a cowboy named Todd Duncan would right this minute be kicking out his last moments at the end of someone's hard-twist lariat, suspended from a cottonwood limb.

This kind of thinking made Duncan's cigarette taste acid. He killed it and looked up to find Berryhill's level gray gaze upon him.

"Doesn't taste so good, does it?" said the lawman. He looked away. "Tom, you and Jack saddle Swindin's horse and tie him across it. The rest of you bring in our horses from out where we left 'em, and let's be heading back."

The others moved away obediently, leaving Duncan and Berryhill looking across the little fire at each other. "Parton," said the lawman softly, "bad enough to be a stranger hereabouts, but if you think you can lie your way out of hanging in Leesville, you're dead wrong."

"Sheriff, if you're so certain I'm Parton, why don't you let 'em do it now. They want to, especially that youngest one."

"Because there's a right way and a wrong way."

Duncan smiled frostily. "Not to a dying man there isn't. If we ride back to your town, that's only stretching it out a little. If there's a trial, that only prolongs it some more."

"You talk like a man that wants to die, Parton. I don't have anything on you yet, but I will have in another day or two. Maybe one of those that's got a conscience that won't let him rest."

"My conscience," said Duncan, "doesn't bother me in the least, Sheriff, but I'll promise you this . . . if you hang me, yours sure will, for as long as you live."

Berryhill stood up. "I'll say one thing for you, Parton, you're as convincing a liar as I've ever run across."

"And you, Sheriff, are as big a fool as I've ever met up with, if you don't make damned sure who I am before you yank the slack out of that rope."

Berryhill looked wry. "Sure," he said very dryly. "Sure, Parton, only you're forgetting something. We've got that old devil who claims he's your paw in jail. Oh, he did a bang-up job at preaching the Gospel, Parton. Getting everyone from town out there at the riverbank while he roared and banged his table . . . but he didn't move fast enough. When young Tom Black recognized Swindin and shot him, breaking up the express office robbery, half a dozen other people saw you, too. From the back, sure, as you two were racing out of town, but they saw you nevertheless, and like I said, Parton, circumstantial evidence has hung its share of killers in this country."

Duncan stood there staring. Now, that sinking sensation behind his belt was very solid and very real. That scar-faced sheriff meant it. He meant to see Duncan hang. He was marshalling the facts in his mind that would indubitably tie Duncan to the killing of someone named Charley Dudley. He was remembering everything Duncan said and everything here at the cottonwood spring that would look damning to a jury.

The graying, big burly man walked up, his face

slack-looking and solemn. "Matt, we got Swindin loaded and the others are waiting. You ready?"

"Sure, Jack, I'm ready. So is Mister Parton here, aren't you, Mister Parton?"

Duncan said: "No, and if I lived to be a thousand, I doubt if I'd ever be ready for hanging, but I don't have much choice, do I?"

"None," said the burly man. "Not at all, Parton."

They left the cottonwood spring with night down all around them. They rode for an hour with very little talk passed back and forth. Softly bumping along behind the graying, burly man, came the dead outlaw named Swindin. Duncan, considering the hard-eyed men around him, had an illusion that all this was a dream, the kind of a nightmare a man might have after eating half-cooked meat or drinking some of that fiery *aguardiente* they served down in Mexico.

It was too well acted out. Too perfectly planned and executed. Thinking back, he could see how everything he'd done since coming down out of the northward hills had worked toward this situation he was now in. He had avoided that town he'd seen. He'd deliberately done that, and yet with no valid reason really, except that he didn't want to waste more time on the trail. But if he'd gone on into that town—he wouldn't be where he now was. And how to explain to these men why he'd avoided their town? They wouldn't believe him.

Later, at the spring, the two cups, two plates. Even the way he was leaning over the dead outlaw, as though to help him, when those posse men stole upon him in the dark.

The letters might help. Sheriff Berryhill had them. But the trouble was Cliff Bowman, the man who'd written them, was a drifter like Todd Duncan was. If Berryhill tried to get in touch with him, the odds were better than even that Cliff wouldn't even still be in Wyoming.

But this preacher . . . there was Duncan's best hope. He could identify Duncan as not being his son, if indeed the other member of this outlaw gang was this man's son at all.

"Smoke?"

Duncan looked around. Berryhill was offering the makings. Duncan shook his head. "Not in the mood now," he said. "Tell me something, Sheriff, are you plumb certain I'm the other outlaw of that trio?"

Berryhill looped his reins, built his smoke, and lit up before he replied. "One of the hardest parts of my job . . . of any lawman's job, I expect . . . is bein' neutral, Parton. You see, no sheriff or deputy or marshal is ever supposed to do anything but make arrests . . . dead or alive. He's not supposed to take sides nor pass any judgments. But like I said, this is the hardest part. Sure I think you're the other one . . . what am I likely to think? There you were, rendezvousing with Swindin, plain as day."

"Could it be possible, Sheriff, that my name really is Todd Duncan, and I'm just passing through your bailiwick on my way south to New Mexico, looking for work?"

"Sure it's possible, Parton. It's also possible your paw really is a preacher. One thing I'll say for the old devil, he sure knows his Good Book. What *isn't* possible is that Charley Dudley will come back. What else isn't possible is that, if you were this Duncan fellow you stole those letters from, and were just passing through, that you'd not ride on into Leesville, because, you see, northward from here there's not a damned town for a long week of riding . . . now you tell me this mythical Duncan or any other cowboy this side of heaven for that matter . . . after not being in a town for eight or nine days . . . would avoid one."

Duncan wagged his head back and forth saying nothing back to Sheriff Berryhill. It was uncanny, how this thing had wrapped him up, tossed him down, and left him there to be six-gun-branded, marked with the indelible brand of the outlaw.

He had friends. A man didn't work the ranges from Montana to Mexico and not make friends. Some of them, like Cliff Bowman for instance, would ride the full distance down to Arizona to help him out of this mess, too. All he'd need to be cleared, he told himself, was some sworn identification. He turned to Berryhill again.

"Tell me, Sheriff, how long before this trial you talked of begins?"

"Tomorrow morning."

Duncan's eyes slowly widened. Berryhill saw this and shrugged. "What's the point in delaying things, Parton? The feeling in town is pretty high. If I tried to postpone things, I just damned well might have a lynch mob to face and I sure don't want that, not in Leesville where I know every-one."

"Oh," said Duncan, "sure not, Sheriff. Hell, a man wouldn't want to jeopardize a few friend-ships over a little thing like maybe hanging the wrong man."

Berryhill blew out a gray cloud and watched it disintegrate in the overhead gloom. "You stick to that story," he said. "Maybe Jack Thorne didn't like it, but I see it as your only way out. Not good enough, Parton, not good enough by a country mile, but, still, it's all you've got. Tell me . . . is that why you always stayed out at the riverside camp and away from town . . . so if anything went wrong, no one could positively identify you as one of them?"

Duncan didn't answer. He drew forth his own tobacco sack and went to work. This was incredible; it was absolutely unbelievable. If anyone had ever put into a novel what was happening to him right now, and if Duncan had read it, he would have flung the novel aside as being just too impossible for belief. How could circumstances dovetail so perfectly, so coincidentally and so totally believably, in a thousand years, to bring about what was now happening to him? The answer was they couldn't. Just maybe once in a thousand years they might.

He lit up, broke the match, and dropped it.

Damned if he didn't have to be the one they ganged up on, too, in that once-in-a-thousand-years interweaving.

CHAPTER THREE

Leesville was that easterly town Duncan had seen in the late afternoon when he'd passed downcountry from the northward hills. It was a pretty little town, quite different from most cow towns. It didn't look as though it had been hurriedly knocked together to serve a quick need by rough men. It even had trees along Main Street, a few genuine brick buildings, and an air of leisurely living that was foreign to every cow town Todd Duncan had ever been in.

But it had one thing the other cow towns had. It possessed its share of bitter-eyed men. Duncan saw them lining the boardwalks as Sheriff Berryhill and his four posse men slowly paced their way through the soft night, alternately passing through orange squares of spilling lamplight and sooty darkness. It also had an atmosphere of raw violence, obviously the aftermath of some very recent unpleasantness that had touched the lives of every one of those motionlessly standing, hard-eyed people gazing without a word at the returning posse.

Berryhill's jailhouse was one of those sturdy brick buildings. It sat between a large mercantile establishment and a wagon works. Here, as Duncan stepped down, townsmen congregated, still saying nothing, still wearing their cruel masks.

Berryhill went ahead, opened the jailhouse door, and roughly called: "All right folks, all right! Step back, out there! We got him and for now that'll be enough."

"Yeah!" someone cried out. "Enough for tonight . . . but not enough for tomorrow. I volunteer for jury duty, Matt."

Duncan was prodded ungently from behind. He twisted, met the mirthless, cold grin of young Tom Black, and started ahead. The other posse men trooped along beside him, burly Jack Thorne on his immediate right. Thorne looked over, saw Duncan's smoothed-out, tight expression, and murmured: "They got a right to feel this way . . . what'd you expect?"

Inside the jailhouse, Berryhill motioned Duncan to a battered table. "Empty your pockets," he ordered. While Duncan was doing this, Berryhill said to the others: "Much obliged for the help, boys. You can go now. I'll put in for your pay with the town council. Jack, stay a minute, will you?"

The others departed and young Tom Black, last to pass over to the door, turned and smiled at Duncan. "Sleep good!" he called over. "Swindin's sleepin' good. He's got me to thank for that."

Thorne closed the street side door after young Black and stood there watching while Matt

Berryhill rifled through Duncan's belongings. "Anything?" he asked.

Berryhill shook his head. "Just the usual." He lifted his head. "Want to see your paw?" he asked.

Duncan said dryly: "I'd sure like that, Sheriff."

Berryhill moved across to a heavy oaken door, jerked his head, and waited. Duncan crossed the room with Jack Thorne's massive bulk bearing down behind him. The three of them passed on into the cell-block where a lamp hung overhead smoking steadily from an untrimmed wick, its glass mantle gray enough to obscure nearly everything its light touched down upon.

Berryhill took Duncan's arm, steered him southward to the farthest cell, half swung him around, and halted. Inside this cell was a great, gaunt old grizzled man with wild eyes and an unkempt beard. Even under different circumstances this character would have arrested Duncan's attention.

"There he is," Sheriff Berryhill said, leaving doubt in Duncan's mind whether Berryhill was addressing him, or that rugged old individual behind the bars.

The gaunt old man stepped forth, put his big bony fists around the bars, and peered intently out at Duncan.

Thorne, his eyes fixed upon the old man, said: "Told you we'd get him, didn't I, you old devil?

Somethin' else you might like to know, too . . . Swindin is dead. That bullet Tom Black put in him from behind killed him. He was dead when we found him . . . and your son here . . . eight miles south of town."

That fierce-eyed old man with his hawkish, high-bridged nose and his awry beard, listened, stared hard at Duncan for a moment, then gradually smiled, all without saying a word until Berryhill stepped away, tinkled some keys, and opened the adjoining cell.

Then the old man said, half chuckling: "I got to hand it to you boys, you're better'n I figured you'd be. So Jerry's dead is he . . . well now, that's too bad. But then Jerry always was impetuous, never could wait and do things right."

"Like killin' that express clerk," growled big Jack Thorne. "You damned old reprobate, you. If I had my way, I'd take you out of there . . . you and your boy . . . and let the town have you both."

"Well, now," said the caged man, his raffish, seamed, and ugly old face lighting up with irony, "how was my boy to know that expressman wasn't reachin' for a weapon when he threw down on him?"

Thorne continued to stare at old Parton for a long time before he shifted his glance past Duncan to Sheriff Berryhill. "That answer enough for you," he asked, "about which one shot Charley?"

Berryhill, standing beside the opened cell door,

nodded. He was staring coldly at Duncan. "It's all the answer I need, Jack. All the answer I wanted. You there, young Parton, get in here."

Duncan's insides felt like ice. He stared at that old man. "What are you doing?" he asked, fighting the panic in him. "What are you trying to do to me, old man? You know damned well we've never before set eyes on one another."

The old man nodded, his face turned sad, turned believably sympathetic. He said: "All right, son, all right. Don't fret now. They're a long way from makin' any of this stick on us."

Berryhill jerked his head and Jack Thorne reached forth, caught Duncan fiercely by the arm, and propelled him inside the adjoining cage. Duncan stood there, looking incredulously out where Berryhill was fastening the lock into place. "Listen," he said to Berryhill and Thorne. "Listen to me a minute, will you?"

"It's late," said the lawman, straightening up and turning, "and I'm dog-tired. Besides that though, I'm up to here with listening to you, Parton. Go to sleep."

He and Jack Thorne moved off. Duncan watched them go out into the other room, close and bar that big oaken door, and he heard their faint footfalls yonder. He turned at a slight rustling sound and saw that evil, ugly old bearded face again, this time up close to their solitary barred wall.

"You damned old devil," swore Duncan. "Why didn't you tell them I wasn't your son? Why did you let them . . . ?"

"You think I want them to run my boy down?" broke in the older man. "Of course not. This way they'll find out you ain't him . . . but by the time they do, my boy'll be plumb out of the country."

That bearded old raffish face split into a slow, fierce smile. "You'll be out one night's sleep under the stars is all, and that sure ain't much to pay to save a fellow man's life now, is it?"

Duncan moved across and the old man stepped gingerly clear of their mutually shared strap-steel wall. He put up a gnarled finger and wagged it back and forth. "No call to be mad now, boy, no cause at all. A little inconvenience ain't much price to pay for your fellow men. Maybe you'd best do like the sheriff said . . . get some sleep."

Duncan stopped with both hands hooked savagely around that cold, unrelenting steel. "You don't know!" he exclaimed. "This isn't near as simple as you think it is, old man. They found me leaning over that Swindin fellow. I'd laid out two cups and two plates. They thought I was your boy. The evidence against me is as tall as a cussed mountain."

The old man wouldn't be convinced of this. He shook his head, went over to a pallet, and sank down there. "Now, how can they prove you were one of us? No way under the sun."

"No? Dammit all, you old fool, I'm in this cell beside you, aren't I?"

"Come daylight, they'll work out the other set of tracks, cowboy. By that time my lad'll be out of their reach and they'll have to turn you loose."

Duncan ran this through his mind. It made sense. In fact, the sheriff had said they'd considered following that other set of tracks but, because Swindin had been shot and couldn't last, they decided to follow him instead. He released the cell straps, fished for his tobacco sack, and went to work manufacturing a smoke. In the morning he'd get Matt Berryhill to run out those other tracks like the old preacher said. He lit up, exhaled, and hadn't felt so good since the day before when he'd had no idea a town such as Leesville even existed.

"Too bad," muttered the old man from his propped-up position in the next cell. "Too bad that tomfool express clerk had to go and get heroic. Why, do you know, boy, there's over sixty thousand dollars in that cussed office? Me and my lads been keepin' even with that money ever since they shipped it south from Fargo. It's been a real trial to us, too. Right up to the moment they unloaded here in Leesville, there's been more shotgun guards standin' over that money box than a man'd ever figure'd be guarding it." The old man's bent fingers went placidly upward and fell to combing his full and unkempt beard. "It's been a real tribulation to us for a fact. Don't y'know my boy even stopped one over at Sioux Pass tryin' to waylay one of the southbound coaches."

Something fell into place in Duncan's mind. He swung to regard the old man. "He got shot?" he asked.

"Yep, smack dab through the right shoulder, neat as a whistle."

"That's why he stayed down at the riverbank," Duncan said, making a statement of this. "That's why these people never got a real close look at him, isn't it?"

"Of course, boy, of course. How would it look for a preacher of salvation to be consortin' with a fellow who'd went and got himself all shot up?"

"How tall was he?" asked Duncan.

"Tall as you are, boy." Those sly old eyes turned, whipped upward over Duncan, slyly smiled through the sootily lighted cell-block, and looked away again. "You're the spittin' image of my boy except in the face . . . and the minute I heard Berryhill and that Thorne fellow call you my boy, I knew they didn't know the difference. Yes, sir . . . except for the face, you could pass as my boy any day in the year."

The old man sat there stroking his beard, smiling with his eyes, and seemingly completely at peace with himself.

"You're going to tell them different though, in the morning," Duncan said.

The stroking stopped. "Why should I? Like I already told you, my boy's got his hurt shoulder. He'll need at least two days' head start to get plumb out of the country."

"You damned old scoundrel," swore Duncan. "They're going to hold a trial tomorrow."

"Trial?" said the old man. "What trial? I didn't shoot that expressman."

"Neither did I."

"Then what's to worry about, cowboy?"

"I'm worrying. The way those men acted who brought me in, they'd play a fiddle for me to do a rope dance with."

"You," intoned the old man softly. "You, boy, not me. That there's the difference. They figure you shot that Dudley fellow, not me."

"You made them think that, damn you!"

"Well now, of course I did. I had to. Jerry Swindin's dead. I been right here in jail, and at the time of the shootin' I was holdin' a camp meetin' at the riverbank, which left only you to be used to get me clear. With my son safely away, cowboy, my only thought is to also get clear. So you see, I had to sort of help 'em to believe what they wanted to believe."

"Parton," Duncan muttered softly. "If I get out of this alive, I'm going to hunt down you and that boy of yours and shoot the pair of you."

The old man turned so that some of that smoky light struck his hawk-like, bony old gaunt face. For the first time Duncan saw his eyes as they really were—sly and ice-cold and completely merciless.

"I already figured you'd feel that way," he said. "That's why I'm going to swear you into that hang rope noose, cowboy. I'll give 'em the evidence they plain want to hear at that blamed trial tomorrow, just so's you won't be able to come after me and my boy. You see, in my business, a fellow's got to be constantly thinkin' ahead for all the angles."

Under Duncan's stricken gaze the old man turned upon his side, slid down, and pillowed his shaggy old head upon one arm with his back to Duncan. He murmured: "Good night, cowboy, sweet dreams."

Duncan didn't move until his cigarette stung his fingers. He flung the thing down, stepped upon it, and half turned to gaze out the tiny, narrow barred window in the back wall of his cell.

He just could not believe it. His one chance for life had turned out to be without doubt the most thoroughly evil person Duncan had ever met in thirty years of life.

He went to his own pallet, sank down upon it, punched at the straw filling until he'd made places for hips and shoulders, then lay there, more awake in the middle of the night than he'd ever been.

CHAPTER FOUR

Morning brought with it several developments. The first one was a female visitor, Marianne Dudley, the dead expressman's daughter. Berryhill brought her in to view Duncan and the pair of them stood outside his cage looking stonily unrelenting.

The girl was very handsome. She was tall and sturdy with taffy-blonde hair and clear blue eyes. There was a fullness to her that sang across the barred intervening distance to Duncan even before Berryhill dryly explained to Duncan who she was. He would have guessed anyway, though, for her stare was cruel and her stance hostile.

"I hope," she told Duncan crisply, after they had exchanged a long look at one another, "I hope you hang. I hope they make your father watch you die."

Duncan had no chance to say a word. Marianne Dudley turned and hastened out of the cell-block into the front jailhouse office.

Sheriff Berryhill lingered to mutter: "Breakfast will be along directly. Thorne's gone for it." He looked at old Parton in the next cell, who was sitting relaxed, watching all this from interested, sardonic eyes. "Maybe you'll get to watch it at that," he said. "That's not a bad idea."

When Berryhill left, Duncan turned, found those fiercely sly old eyes upon him, and ran an unsteady hand over the beard stubble on his face. The old man fell to combing that wild gray beard of his with bent fingers.

"A fine lookin' specimen of a female," he stated. "A right sturdy heifer if I ever saw one. What do you say, boy?"

Duncan kept his back to old Parton. "I say I'm getting a sort of constricting feeling around my throat, you damned old devil," he muttered. Then he turned to regard the old man through their steel bar partition. "Listen, if they'll hold off their trial until tomorrow, will you tell the truth?"

Old Parton continued to stroke his beard while he ran this through his mind. "They won't hold off," he said finally. "Listen to the noise out in the roadway, boy. These here good citizens are all fired up. Why, this is like a big celebration to 'em. You're wishin' for the moon. If the law was to try and postpone your trial, son, there'd be a lynch mob around this here jailhouse quicker'n you could say scat."

Duncan crossed over to stand beneath that narrow overhead barred window where morning sunlight came downward as a golden shaft to add the only mote of cheerfulness to this otherwise dingy, demoralizing gray world. He could hear roadway traffic and the brisk beat of many booted feet upon the plank walks around front. He could hear men calling back and forth, their voices ringing with vigor and anticipation. He couldn't make out many of their sung-out words, but he didn't have to, the feeling was there unmistakably. Old Parton was correct; Leesville was up early today. It was rushing about its normal affairs in order to have free time when court convened. There was an air of jubilant expectation in the air, an unmistakable attitude of righteous vengeance.

He twisted to look around as someone passed into the cell-block from Berryhill's office. This was Jack Thorne, Berryhill's burly big companion. Thorne was now wearing a deputy's badge pinned to his shirt front. He brought two bowls of mush and two tin cups of black coffee. He scarcely looked at Duncan but he pushed old Parton's breakfast under the steel door with almost a solicitous examination of the older man.

Parton made a wan, resigned face, and Duncan, watching the old man, very gradually came to the sickening realization that old Parton was an accomplished actor. Without speaking a word or even moving, he was projecting for Thorne's benefit an image of grieving fatherhood. He sat in there all crouched low upon his pallet making no move to take either his bowl of mush or his cup of coffee.

Thorne dropped his glance from the old man's face, shuffled over, and pushed Duncan's food in at him. Here Jack Thorne's glance hardened against this cell's inmate. When he straightened up again, he said through lips that scarcely moved: "I'll fetch you some soap and water. No sense in you walkin' into the courtroom lookin' like that."

"And a razor," said Duncan, wildly thinking on the spur of the moment he might be able to accomplish something with a razor in his hands.

But Thorne's lips pulled down in a mirthless smile. "Sure," he said. "Maybe you'd rather I just brought you a couple of guns." And he left.

Old Parton cocked his head, listened to someone lock the oaken door from beyond it, then swooped down upon his breakfast and ravenously consumed the mush. Duncan, who had no appetite, not even for the coffee, watched as the old man straightened up, coffee cup in one bony hand, sniffed the bouquet of that oily black beverage, and rolled his eyes over at Duncan.

"Eat, boy," Parton said. "You're goin' to need all the strength you got." Parton sipped, sucked droplets from the corner of his beard with a bubbly sound and gently bobbed his shaggy head up and down. "Man can't put up much show on an empty belly, son. You'd better eat up."

Duncan slumped. It was not warm in the cell-block but he had sweat running under his shirt. He kept watching old Parton, half wondering if there was some way to reach him, half wishing he could get into the old man's cell for five minutes.

"Well, then," Parton spoke up again. "If you don't want the mush how about passin' it through the bars. Sittin' around in here makes me hungry as a bitch wolf."

Duncan's frustration increased. He stepped off the width of his cell, stepped off the length of it, spun at the completion of his last circuit and found the old man standing there, peering at him through the bars, his bushy beard and shadowed face giving him the appearance of some ancient patriarch of Biblical times.

"What would it take to make you tell the truth?" Duncan asked. "Tell me that much, Parton."

"Well now, boy . . . if they'd hold off sentencin' you until tomorrow, and if they'd give me amnesty and free passage out of their stinkin' little town, why then I'd gladly tell 'em how it really was."

Old Parton began negatively to wag his head. He kept this up all the time he resumed speaking, as though powerfully to emphasize his next words.

"But you know they wouldn't do that, boy. They'll convene their court by noon. They'll hear you and me and a half dozen of their own stupid people by two o'clock. They'll sentence you by three and hang you by four. By the way, when you come into town, did they fetch you in the back way? No? Well, you missed seein' the gibbet. It's a little weathered, but it's solid built. It stands just west of town."

39

"Would you really go through with it, Parton . . . seeing me hang knowing what you know in your heart?"

The old man didn't answer this. He didn't have to. As soon as Duncan asked it, he saw his answer in those fierce, merciless old sunk-set pale eyes. Parton would go through with it. Better than that, he would act out the part of the anguished father right up to the last, exactly as Duncan had briefly glimpsed him acting it out for Jack Thorne a short while earlier.

The second event of this fateful morning occurred when Matthew Berryhill came in with a tired-looking elderly priest beside him. The holy man glanced only very briefly at Parton, but in that fleeting second Duncan saw such a degree of distaste on the priest's wrinkled face it jarred him away from his own immediate predicament for a moment.

Then Berryhill spoke. "This is the young one, Father," he said to the priest. "The one who killed Charley."

That old priest nodded, glanced steadily in at Duncan, saying nothing for a while, then nodded again and turned. "Leave me with him, Matt," he said. "I'll knock when I want back out."

Berryhill walked away without so much as a glance at Duncan. He closed and barred the oaken door from without.

For a little while the old priest simply gazed in

at Duncan. He had a way of putting his aged eyes upon a man as though commiserating with him, and yet Duncan thought he detected a shrewd and assessing appraisal going on all the time this deceptively mild old gaze was fixed upon him. He wanted to feel hope, to view this rickety old priest as some kind of an omen, but Duncan was a practical, forthright man, not only with others but with himself, also. That old man looking in at him in his dusty, unpressed black suit, his cracked old shoes, his frayed cuffs and skeletal hands clasped over a caved-in, emaciated middle, was far from hope inspiring. He seemed more like some toothless old bird of prey hovering beyond Duncan's bars, waiting as buzzards habitually wait.

Parton broke the silence with a cackle. "A fellow brother of the cloth," he said. "Aye, but a popist . . . and from the looks of him a lifelong one at that."

The priest ignored Parton with a disdain too deep for description. He said to Duncan: "The daughter of the man you shot asked me to see you." At Duncan's quick look of surprise the priest inclined his head. "I know . . . I know what she said to you. That's what made her come to me. Still, whether you can forgive her or not, I'm sure, after seeing you, that you can understand why she said that about wishing you would hang and that your father be forced to watch."

Duncan stepped over to the bars, raised both hands, and hooked them there. "You're not going to believe this any more than anyone else does, Father, but I'm not that old devil's son, and I didn't shoot anyone named Charley Dudley, and I've never before been in this town in my life."

The priest's soft milky stare lingered upon Duncan's haggard face for a long time. For a moment Duncan thought he spied a little break of interest in that gaze, but it was gone too soon for him to be sure.

"All right, my boy," retorted the elderly holy man, using the mild, indulgent tone one used with children. "All right. I'm willing to accept that. But let me point out to you, lad, that you're unknown here, the facts seem to warrant a strong belief in a different view of things, and unless you have some excellent proof of innocence, man's law is going to prevail here today. Now tell me, lad, have you such proof?"

Duncan felt old Parton's glittering eyes upon him from the gloom of the adjoining cell. Old Parton was listening to this exchange carefully. It required no great divination for Duncan to understand why this was. Parton, ready to swear Duncan's life away in a courtroom, wanted to know everything he could that Duncan might say in order to have his own solid rebuttals ready.

Duncan shook his head. "No proof, Father," he

mumbled. "I rode over the northward hills into this country a perfect stranger. I saw two cottonwood trees, knew there'd be a spring, rode over, and found that dead man . . . that Jerry Swindin. The rest of it you've probably already heard from Sheriff Berryhill."

"Yes, I've heard it. Not only from Matthew Berryhill but also from the posse men who were with him when they found you. Tell me something . . . is there anyone I can telegraph to in your behalf?"

"I have no folks, Father."

"I see. How about friends?"

"Sure, dozens of 'em from Canada to Mexico. But without a postponement of this trial that's getting under way, you'd only get the telegrams sent . . . you'd never get the answers back in time."

"Amen," intoned old Parton, wickedly smiling through the bars. "Amen, Dominie. The lad's got a good head on him, hasn't he?" Parton broadly smiled, cocked his head making a raffish wink, and said: "Gets it from my side of the family, he does. All the Partons was clever folks . . . all of 'em."

The priest waited out this interruption without looking at Parton, without letting on by facial expression that Parton even existed. "Do you know anything about this other man . . . this one you say you have been mistaken for?"

"No, only what that old whiskered devil's told me. He was shot in the shoulder trying to rob a stage up north somewhere. That's why Parton's willing to swear under oath I'm his son . . . to give his real son time enough to get plumb away. He can't travel hard with a bad shoulder. He'll need rest from time to time. He said if the trial could be held off for one more day though, he'd tell the truth and get me off, in exchange for amnesty."

For the first time the old priest turned towards Parton. From a face as blank as hewn stone he said: "Will you do that if there is a postponement for one day?"

Parton rolled his eyes. He looked sadly over at Duncan and spoke in a low, roughened tone: "Dominie, the boy's inclined to imagine things. It's the strain. He's been denyin' his own pappy ever since they brought him in. Of course I never said no such a thing. How could I? I'm his pappy and he shot that expressman. It grieves me to the marrow to see my own flesh and blood tryin' to use his old pappy to worm out of this mess."

Parton turned with dragging steps, crossed over to his pallet, and sank down there. He began combing his beard again, began to sadly wag his leonine old head and softly sniffle.

"I know how it is with you, Dominie," he said. "You despise us itinerant preachers of salvation. And I'll confess it's a hard, unrewardin' life for a

44

fact. But when a man gets the call . . ." Parton lifted and dropped his bony shoulders. "The Lord's will be done."

Duncan's anger rose up nearly choking him. "You damned old hypocrite," he swore. "You lousy faker, Parton. You use that preaching of yours to cover up a heart as black as sin. I'd trade five years off my life to get into that cell with you for five minutes. You'd tell the truth. . . . Damned if you wouldn't!"

CHAPTER FIVE

Sheriff Berryhill brought two tin basins and some water. He watched Duncan wash from a leaning position across the narrow corridor outside the cells. As Duncan was finishing, he said: "In case it's worrying you, Parton, we got a sort of lawyer to represent you."

Duncan looked up. "What is a 'sort of' lawyer, Sheriff, someone you appointed?"

Berryhill nodded. "Yup. Leesville's got no regular lawyers and we won't have time to import any."

"And the judge," asked Duncan. "Is he a 'sort of' judge, too?"

Berryhill's voice turned a little sharp at this sarcasm. "You can say that if you like, Parton, but one thing I'll tell you, he's hung his share of renegades. He's the local liveryman. His name is Walter Sheay. Two years back the folks hereabouts petitioned the territorial legislature to appoint him justice court judge for this district."

Duncan finished with the towel, tossed it aside, and ran both hands through his heavy mane of chestnut hair. "It's cut and dried, though," he said, looking straight out at Berryhill. "Isn't it, Sheriff?"

There was no reply to this question. Berryhill

nodded at the tin basin. "Push it back under the door," he ordered. As Duncan stooped to obey, the sheriff said dispassionately: "The punishment for murder usually is cut and dried in folks' minds, Parton. You've been around enough to know that. You should've thought about it a little before you pulled that trigger."

Duncan finished with the basin, straightened up, and leaned on the cell door. "You know, Sheriff," he said quietly, "if anyone had told me there were people in this country as hypocritical as you are, and as just plain stupid, I wouldn't have believed them."

Berryhill picked up the basin as though Duncan's words had not affected him. He stepped over to the next cell, growled at its bearded inmate, picked up that basin, too, then turned back to Duncan. As soon as his face came around though, Duncan saw the rusty dark and angry stain in it.

"Mind explainin' that hypocritical remark?" he asked softly.

"You told me on the way into town your job was enforcing the law, not prejudging people, yet there you stand right now with it plain in your face. In your eyes I'm guilty as hell and you'll enjoy seeing me hang. That's what I meant. A man can't say he believes in one thing, then do the exact opposite without being hypocritical, Berryhill."

For a moment the lawman just stood there gazing in at Duncan. He walked up a little closer, balancing those wash basins, and said—"You're a pretty good actor, Parton."—and walked on out of the cell-block.

As the door closed, there was a soft cackle from the adjoining cell that grated on Duncan's nerves. "Boy, I got to hand it to you. Berryhill was mad enough to eat you alive there for a second, but in the next breath you had him doubtin' his own beliefs."

Duncan kept his back to old Parton. He could see where that shaft of sunlight was narrowing a little on the yonder wall outside his cell. It would be about 9:00 a.m., he thought, and wondered what time court would convene.

In the next cell old Parton shuffled about getting some exercise, then he went to his pallet and stretched out there. "How about some of that tobacco you got," he drawled.

Duncan ignored him. He remained motionless against the front of his cage. For some reason he fell to thinking of Marianne Dudley. It was entirely possible that someday she would cross paths with the real murderer of her father and she would never know it.

Of course by that time Todd Duncan wouldn't be around to appreciate the subtle irony of such a meeting.

He turned, paced to the rear wall, stood in that

paling sun shaft gazing upward and outward where a sky of enameled, purest blue shone, tried to reconcile himself fatalistically to what was unavoidably going to happen to him. He was shortly interrupted in this by that thick oaken door swinging open again from up by Berryhill's office. He turned only his head.

Thorne and Berryhill both came into the cell-block. Duncan's heart sank. Those two wooden faces had a doomsday look to them. They had come, he was positive, to escort the prisoners to wherever Duncan's trial was to be held.

Thorne stopped in front of Duncan's cell. Berryhill stopped there, also. He did not pass along to old Parton's cage as Duncan expected him to. Thorne held up a worn cut-away hip holster with a six-gun in it.

"You recognize this?" he asked, watching Duncan's face.

The prisoner crossed over, looked, and nodded. "It's mine," he said. "You know that. You fellows took it off me out at that cottonwood spring."

Thorne lowered the gun. His brows were down a little, making his unwavering gaze look long and faintly puzzled. "How many shots did you and Swindin fire in that shoot-out at the express office?"

Duncan's temper flashed up. "Damn you," he swore at Thorne, "I wasn't there. I didn't shoot any shots, and I'm getting a bellyful of looking at your stupid face and always hearing the same false accusations coming out of it. I haven't shot that gun in at least three months. I can't even remember the last time I fired it."

"Yeah," said Berryhill from his position behind and off to one side of Jack Thorne. "That's what's so interesting. That gun hasn't been fired in a long time. Jack and I both thought so, but to make plumb certain we took it to our local gunsmith. He said the same thing."

Duncan's heart began to pound. He looked closely into those two blank faces. In the next cell he heard old Parton scrambling up off his pallet to come closer where he could hear all this.

"Something else," Berryhill said. "Every loop in this shell belt has a bullet in it . . . an unfired bullet. Of course it's possible for a fellow to carry a few spares loose in his pocket, but it's sure not usual for a man to do that, is it?"

"Those bullets," said Duncan, fighting to keep the excitement and the resurrected hope out of his voice, "are all the slugs I had in the world. If you doubt me, go look in my saddle pockets."

"We already have," Thorne advised him.

"Then you got reason to believe me when I say I had no hand in that expressman's killing." Duncan gripped the bars. "Maybe you'll do something else, too, fellows. Maybe you'll quit standing around here and go out where you told me the trail of those killers parted, forget the one you followed to the cottonwood spring, and make a damned fast ride over the other one. That man you want has a bullet wound in his shoulder. He can't ride hard. Ask his paw in the next cell if that's not so. If you work at it, boys, you'll overtake him. That man is Parton's son, not me, and he's the one who killed your expressman."

Berryhill and Thorne stood like stone, their glances unmoving for a long time. Thorne finally looked at the sheriff, ruefully wagged his head, and said: "You were sure right, Matt. He's the smoothest talker of the bunch. Smoother even than his paw."

Duncan's breathing stopped. His jaw dropped. Those two men out there had never for a minute believed one word he'd said to them. "What . . . ," he blurted out. "What . . . the hell?"

Jack Thorne held up the holstered six-gun again. "One thing about murder," he said, "a man doesn't get hung any higher for killin' two men than he does for killin' one. It's a lousy shame but that's the way it is. . . . Parton, we know where you got this unfired gun and full shell belt." Thorne gestured toward the outside roadway. "The man you took them off is outside in a rancher's wagon . . . stiff as a poker with your slug through his heart from the back."

Duncan hung there on the bars staring at those two. From the adjoining cell he heard a long, bubbly sigh slide past the bearded lips of old Jeremiah Parton.

"We rode that back trail," Thorne said quietly. "We met the cowman comin' along it with his wagon out there. He had this stranger in back, dead like you left him, Parton. We come on back to town with the corpse and that's when we got an answer to the riddle of that unfired gun and full shell belt."

Berryhill's expression turned a little wry, a little bitter.

"You almost had me believin' you this morning, Parton," he said. "You're pretty good at play-actin'. That gun and belt had me really beginnin' to wonder. Jack here, too. There was no place for you to buy fresh shells after you and Swindin lit out of Leesville, and you hardly had time to clean your gun, let alone have the accumulation of dust in its barrel there was in this weapon."

Berryhill stopped speaking. He looked blankly over where old Jeremiah Parton was pressing his face against the bars intently, watching and listening. "You ought to be real proud of him, old man, real proud," he finally continued. "He's not only a cold-blooded back-shooter, but he's also as good an actor as you are."

Sheriff Berryhill drew up, staring in at Duncan. He growled: "Break it off, Jack. Let's get out of here and take that body down to Doc's embalmin' shed. It makes me sick to my stomach seeing that young one actin' so plumb speechless. And *he* had the guts to call *me* a hypocrite."

The two of them walked away. After they'd passed on out of the cell-block, old Parton stepped back, bent double, and nearly choked with restrained laughter. After a moment of this he dashed at the tears in his eyes with a bony fist and gasped out: "Dang it for purest luck. I never seen anything work up against a fellow as neat as all this is workin' up ag'in' you, boy. Never in all my borned days." Parton choked, slapped his leg, and made a little mincing dance step.

"What a brace of complete simpletons those two are. Followed out the trail they said, until they met some old cow nurse with that body in his rig, then turned plumb around and come straight on back, sure as shootin' they knew exactly what happened. Why, good Lord, boy, any lawmen worth their lousy salt wouldn't've split up . . . one comin' back, the other one followin' on down that trail. How do you like that for just plain simple-mindedness?"

Duncan said: "That was your son out there, Parton. He shot that traveler and took his gun and belt."

"Sure, boy, sure. But those two idiots thought when they found that dead man without his gun belt, they had the answer to how come your gun and belt look unused." Parton's bearded lips flew apart in a massive, silent laugh that showed pink wetness where once there had been teeth. He struck his legs again and rocked back and forth in soundless glee. "By gawd . . . damnedest thing I ever heard of. It is for a pure fact, boy." Suddenly the laughter dried up and the ugly old man's gaunt, hawkish face tilted, the eyes turned flatly sly again.

"They're goin' to hang you so high the cussed birds'll be buildin' nests in your hair." Those sly, steely old eyes turned saturnine. "Not that I got a thing against you, boy. It ain't a personal thing at all, you understand. But I'll be damned if the circumstantial evidence isn't buildin' up around you higher'n that gibbet out there. It's downright uncanny, that's what it is."

Duncan was thinking the same thing, but with a different attitude about it. He hung there upon the front bars of his cell until the little old priest appeared, almost noiselessly.

At least Duncan didn't hear him approaching until old Parton said: "You're sure popular this mornin', son. Here's the old bead-roller again."

Duncan looked down into that gray, aged face with its deceptively mild glance. He didn't want to talk to the priest, or to anyone for that matter. He was still numb in his heart and in his mind over what had just occurred between himself and the two lawmen.

The priest murmured a gentle greeting, then said: "I'm afraid you're going to have to wait until this afternoon before they try you, young man."

Duncan's eyes slowly focused on the old priest. That faint though persevering flicker of hope weakly warmed him.

"Why?"

"The judge's down abed with his heart trouble. He's being doctored, though, and they say he'll be well enough later today . . . but not this morning. His niece is with him."

Something caused a flashing premonition to erupt in Duncan's mind. "His niece, Father?"

"Yes. Marianne."

"Father, are you telling me Marianne Dudley is the judge's niece?"

"Aye, lad, she is. Charley Dudley, the man you're accused of killing, was her father. He was also the judge's brother-in-law."

Duncan turned numb all over. He swung his head feebly towards Jeremiah Parton in the next cell. The bearded old renegade was standing there looking out of wide-open eyes at the priest, his mouth slack, his face white from upper lip to forehead.

"Coincidence," Duncan said from cold lips. "You thought that business about the dead man and the gun was purest coincidence. Parton, what do you think of *this?*"

Parton kept staring at the priest. He said nothing.

"The judge is an honest man, son," murmured

the priest. "He'll not judge you dishonestly . . . brother-in-law or no brother-in-law."

"Oh, hell no," muttered Duncan, turning weakly away. "Oh, hell no, Father." He crossed over to his pallet and dropped down there all in a heap.

After a while the priest departed and there was absolute silence in the cell-block. Even old Jeremiah Parton was still.

CHAPTER SIX

Duncan's numbness did not leave him for a long time. He lay there upon his pallet watching that sun shaft climb the forward wall beyond his cell with a kind of apathy holding him tightly in its grip. Even when old Parton asked again for some tobacco he didn't move.

Parton said complainingly: "Listen, boy, that's the way the cards fall. Ain't much sense in bein' all hateful-like about it."

"Shut up!"

"Now put yourself in my boots, boy. You'd do as much if it was your son. Y'know you would."

"You damned old goat!"

"So what's a little tobacco?"

Duncan rolled his head to see if old Parton was sincere in this. He was. At least his expression was droll and relaxed, as though he were discussing something of no very great importance.

"Old man," growled Duncan. "I don't know what it was the Lord left out when He put you together, but whatever it is, I'm sure thankful He didn't leave it out of more folks."

Parton judged this remark thoughtfully before saying: "Son, you ain't ever going to use up all that tobacco, anyway. Why, this time tomorrow I could be rollin' me a smoke out of that sack and sayin' a little prayer over the freshly turned earth you'll be under. Now you just try and name me one other person in this whole of the countryside who'd do that much for you. Name me just one."

Duncan rolled his head away from Parton. Outside somewhere, he heard some whooping cowboys lope into town. There were other sounds to hear, also. This was all he had to occupy himself with unless he continued morbidly to dwell upon that narrowing slot in time that was his own dwindling lifespan.

Some men were hammering westerly from the jailhouse. Abruptly a dog fight erupted outside in the back alley and shrill boyish voices broke out in accompaniment.

Duncan was lying there cataloging all these homely sounds and did not hear the cell-block door open. He was unaware that he and old Parton were not alone until Sheriff Berryhill said from outside: "Parton, I've got to warn you. There's a lot of feeling in town about you."

Duncan rose up, saw Berryhill's uneasy expression, felt something like ice water drip down his spine, and got to his feet as the lawman resumed speaking.

"Folks are put out because the judge had one of his spells. If we could've held the trial like I wanted, early this morning, it'd all be over by now and none of the riders from the outlyin' cow outfits would be ridin' in, tankin' up at the saloons, and talkin' about a lynch party."

Then old Parton got up and padded forward to press his shaggy face against the bars. It was difficult to see expression in his hawkish, hairy face, but Duncan thought Parton had a suddenly alert and concerned expression in his cold eyes.

"You warnin' us, Sheriff?" the old man asked, his voice sharp.

Berryhill nodded, looking dourly from one to the other. "You got a right to know," he stated.

Duncan said: "How bad is it?"

"Not bad yet and I've got Thorne out there trying to talk it down, but these things got a way of snowballing. It's my duty to warn you, just like it's my duty to do everything a man can to prevent trouble."

"How many cowboys, Sheriff?"

Berryhill wagged his head back and forth. "Enough," he muttered. "They're still ridin' in. That's what Jack and I don't like. By afternoon there'll be a sizeable crowd of 'em."

"And the townsmen?" asked Duncan.

"Yeah, a lot of them, too."

"You got a telegraph office in Leesville!" Duncan exclaimed. "What the hell are you waiting for . . . send for U.S. marshals or soldiers."

Berryhill put his skeptical eyes upon Duncan. "How'd you know we had a telegraph office? You told us you'd never been in Leesville in your life, remember?"

"That priest told me," snapped Duncan. He

threw a look at old Jeremiah in the next cell. "Didn't he, Parton?"

"Well now, son, not that I heard, but then maybe he did and I just wasn't listening real good."

Duncan's face gradually got brick red. He'd done it again. He'd walked right into another of the old man's sly traps. He reached forth, gripped the cell bars with both fists, and squeezed until his knuckles showed white from the straining.

Sheriff Berryhill saw this fierce anger, ignored it, and swung all their thoughts back to his particular dilemma by saying: "If worst comes to worst, Jack and I've worked out a way of slippin' you two out the back way and over to the next county for safekeeping. But that's just in case . . . I don't figure we'll have too much trouble until about three o'clock, and by then the judge ought to be feelin' well enough to get court convened. If he does, that'll be the end of this other trouble."

"Yeah," grated Duncan. "It sure will be the end, won't it? Why didn't you tell me your 'sort of' judge was that dead expressman's brother-in-law?"

"I knew what you'd say, that's why. But I'll tell you this . . . I've known Walter Sheay for twenty years. Where the law is concerned, he wouldn't bat an eye at sentencing his own mother."

Duncan let off a big sigh. He kept staring at Berryhill with futility filling him until he could have choked on it. "Why don't you just let 'em hang me?" he said in a dull tone. "Get this damned farce over with."

The husky sheriff nodded faintly with his gaze hardening against Duncan. "If I wasn't behind this badge, Parton, I almost think I might go along with that suggestion. But since I am behind it . . . no lynchings in my town, not even when they deserve it."

Berryhill walked away.

Jeremiah Parton came to Duncan's separating steel partition. He was no longer in his customary raffish, sly, and vicious mood. He looked in at the younger man from very sober and thoughtful eyes.

"You ever seen a lynchin', boy?" he asked. When Duncan neither answered nor faced around, Parton emphatically bobbed his head up and down. "I have, and let me tell you, there's nothin' about 'em to joke over."

Duncan twisted, saw Parton's anxiety plain as day, and for the first time in nearly twenty-four hours he smiled. "Care for some of that tobacco now, you were so plumb sure you'd be smoking over my grave tomorrow?"

"You listen to me, boy, this here ain't funny. There's only that sheriff and his deputized friend out there. And I've seen brick buildings like this one dynamited before."

Duncan went right on smiling. "Hell, old man,

you wanted to buy your boy some time. I can't think of a better way than by you doing the rope dance beside me tonight."

Parton shot Duncan a venomous look, swung around, and began pacing across his cell. He continued to pace for some time, occasionally halting to cock his head in a listening fashion, before he would begin to cover the distance of floor again.

Duncan worked up a smoke, lit it, and blew smoke toward that high little barred window in the rear wall. "I'm feeling better for the first time since they tossed me in here," he said loudly, catching old Parton's attention and holding it with this loud talk. "It's unreal how all those things piled up against me, but, by golly, I think some of that black luck is rubbing off on you now, and I sure like that, Parton. I do for a fact."

"All they got on me," snarled the old man, "is that my boy and Jerry Swindin tried to get the express office money cache. I wasn't in on it and they can't prove otherwise."

Duncan's smile deepened, his frosty stare brightened, turned sardonic and cruel. "Parton, you just try and tell that to a lynch mob. There'll be so much shouting going on when those drunken range riders bust in here, you could shoot a cannon and no one'd hear it. Besides, all those lynchers have to know is that you're in here. That's all. Old man, they'll stretch your scrawny neck until they can read a newspaper through it."

Parton swore at Duncan, using savage profanity for the first time. He went to the back wall, stood there, head cocked for a moment, then shuffled back toward the front of his cell again.

"You think this is funny," he snarled. "Go back there and listen. That bunch out there ain't goin' to wait until this here judge gets his pump back in workin' order. Go on . . . go back there and listen."

Duncan didn't go. He leaned upon his cell door, smoking and slowly losing his smile. He'd extricated all the grim pleasure he wished to out of this perilous situation, and turned next to wondering just how much of a chance Berryhill and Thorne would have at eluding a town full of half-drunk, excited cowboys and townsmen. He came eventually to the conclusion that the time factor was likely to prove important, perhaps even critical. Thorne and the sheriff could not hope to leave town with their two prisoners in broad daylight and he doubted very much, judging from the solid and increasing racket out front, if they could pre-vent trouble until after dark, when it would perhaps be safe to try and spirit their prisoners away.

He dropped his smoke, stepped upon it, shot a careless glance over at old Parton, crossed his cell to the rear wall, and leaned there. At once the old man said loudly: "Hear that? Well, you still think it's funny?"

Duncan inclined his head. "It keeps getting funnier, you old goat. I've got nothing to lose. They're going to hang me anyway. That's been tickling you since last night. Now it's my turn to smile a little."

"Blessed little," growled old Parton. "Why don't that damned sheriff do like you said . . . send for some soldiers or some U.S. marshals?"

"That reminds me," said Duncan. "Thanks for helping me out about that telegraph office."

"By gawd, I'll tell 'em I'm no relation to you . . . that you killed their expressman on your own."

"No good, Parton. You've already put on your act for both Berryhill and Thorne. It was real good play-acting, too. I could've strangled you then, but now I think I'll just start calling you paw. In fact, if we get a chance to say anything just before they yank us, I'll tell 'em you planned that job from start to finish. I'll even say you told me to kill that expressman."

Parton put up a hand and began swiftly, agitatedly to comb his beard. He crossed to his pallet, gazed down at it, turned, and took another three steps and listened at the back wall again.

Duncan lay down, tilted up his hat, and closed his eyes. He didn't feel at all like sleeping, and actually old Parton was right. There wasn't anything funny about those increasing catcalls outside at all. But he wanted to think and this was the best way.

He rummaged among all the things that had happened to him in the last twenty-four hours for some logical explanation of how so many coincidences could dovetail around him so perfectly. He also thought back to everything that had been said between him and Sheriff Berryhill or Jack Thorne, which might give him some clue as to how—if that mob out there didn't get him—he might still come out of this alive.

"Hey," Parton breathed sharply, suddenly. "Get up . . . someone's coming."

Duncan eased back his hat, looked up the corridor, saw Berryhill approaching with two tin trays, and arose. The sheriff pushed Parton's tray under his door and moved to do the same for Duncan. He said not a word and his expression was grimly and tightly locked. Parton bombarded him with questions, seared him with insults and imprecations, and wheedled at him in a whining tone that inspired Duncan to say: "Shut up! You got a yellow streak up your back a yard wide."

Parton went quiet but his cold old eyes never once moved off Sheriff Berryhill, who raised up from pushing Duncan's tray in to him, and said: "You don't hear so good, do you?"

"Good enough," snapped Duncan. "You and that old goat over there got your guts running out your feet. I've heard mobs before."

"Well, if you had a lick of sense, you'd be afraid of this one," rapped out Berryhill. "There are close to a hundred men out there. Most of them have been drinkin' steadily now for two hours. By three o'clock, if Walt Sheay isn't on the bench in his courtroom . . ." Berryhill gravely wagged his head back and forth without finishing his last sentence, his steady gaze never departing from Duncan's countenance.

"Hey, Sheriff, listen to me a minute," Parton nearly shouted. "You got to send for help. That's your job . . . protectin' your prisoners. You got to send . . ."

"Parton," cut in the lawman harshly, "you should've made a better study of this countryside before you settled here to rob the express office. The nearest Army post is four days' ride from here and the nearest marshal is six hundred miles away. Even if they could fly like a bird couldn't any of them get here fast enough."

Right after Berryhill said this someone out front hurled a large rock against the jailhouse street-side wall. This impact reverberated through the entire building.

Parton jumped. "Sheriff, you got to arm us. We got a right to protect ourselves. Sheriff, Sheriff . . ."

Berryhill was walking away. He turned, passed beyond sight, and a moment later Duncan heard the bar drop behind that massively separating oak door.

"You're a preacher," Duncan said to Parton. "Now's the time to get down on your prayer bones and start working up a miracle."

CHAPTER SEVEN

Duncan had no very exact idea of the time when that outside racket began suddenly and audibly to increase, but he thought it had to be close to 3:00 p.m. He got up, walked over to the back wall, and stood there considering those catcalling, derisive outcries coming around to him from the front roadway.

In his adjoining cell Jeremiah Parton's forehead was visibly shiny and his talon-like hands, instead of combing that bushy old gray beard, were now twisting it.

Duncan heard a rattle of stones strike the jailhouse from out front. He turned to see Parton's reaction to this. The old man was standing with his legs wide-planted and his head forward, straining to hear. He very clearly did not believe Berryhill and Thorne would be able to keep out that ugly mob. He turned, saw Duncan standing over there watching him, and shook his shaggy head.

"Bad," he muttered. "It's bad out there, boy. I don't like this even a little bit."

"You'll like it less when they bust in here, Parton."

"Damn you!" screeched the old man, suddenly coming unwound and whipping upright, facing

Duncan. "Damn you for a fool. I tell you they're goin' to get inside. Beat on your bars, get someone in here to set us loose and give us arms. We got a right to protect ourselves . . . that's the cussed law."

"Naw," Duncan replied, still calm, still watching old Parton's agitation with clinical interest. "That's not the law here, I can tell you that right now. Berryhill doesn't care. He told me on the ride in, he knew these people too well to fight them over someone like me."

"He didn't," croaked Parton.

Duncan nodded. "Wait and see."

Almost as though this were a cue for his entrance, Sheriff Berryhill appeared in the cell-block. He was carrying a sawed-off, double-barreled shotgun. Standing back in the doorway, which led into the outer office, stood Jack Thorne, also armed with a riot gun.

Berryhill came along briskly, shot Duncan a look, and halted at old Parton's cell to put aside his shotgun, insert a key, and swing back Parton's cell door.

"Out!" he snapped.

Parton moved with surprising alacrity. Heretofore Duncan had seem him only as a shuffling, aged renegade. Now he saw this other side of that old man's character. Parton halted with his back to Berryhill, staring at that leaning shotgun.

Duncan said casually: "Watch him, Sheriff. That was a tomfool thing to do . . . to leave that shotgun like that."

Berryhill looked up and around, put out a thick arm to push off old Parton, then scooped up the gun and wordlessly stepped along to Duncan's cell.

"Go on up front," he ordered Parton. "Up where Jack is. Get any more silly ideas and I'll feed you to those wolves out there."

Parton was hiking toward Thorne when Berryhill flung back Duncan's door and jerked his head. Duncan walked out, turned, and struck out after Parton.

At the doorway, Thorne, looking grim as death, stepped back, brusquely motioned both prisoners into the outer office, and waited for Berryhill to come along before he closed and barred that cell-block door again.

In Berryhill's office it became instantly apparent to Duncan and Parton why the two lawmen were so grim and hair-triggered. In the outside road-way a mob of hooting, stone-throwing, cursing men milled aimlessly in front of the jailhouse. There was one small, barred window Duncan could peer through to see that mob. They were mostly cow-boys. There were some townsmen, too, but not nearly as many as there were range men.

Parton stepped over beside Duncan, craned for a look out, swung away as a stone broke the window, and flinched at the tinkling sound of falling glass.

Berryhill and Thorne looked up at the sound of the breaking glass. Thorne went forward as though to poke his shotgun barrel out at the crowd but Berryhill sang out at him in a sharp way, halting Thorne in his tracks.

"Don't make 'em any madder," cautioned the sheriff. "It's five o'clock. We've got to keep 'em neutralized a couple hours longer before it'll be dark."

Duncan looked inquiringly over where Berryhill was chucking shotgun loads from a rumpled cardboard box into a shirt pocket.

"What about the trial?" he asked.

"That," growled Thorne, turning back and spearing Duncan with a cold stare, "will be postponed a while longer. Judge Sheay's not up to sitting on the bench yet." Thorne's mighty shoulders rolled up, his stare became truculent, and his large hands curled into fists. "You two Partons are goin' to get some good men hurt tonight, I think, and what roils me is that the pair of you together isn't worth the hand off one of those men out there."

Berryhill put a disapproving look upon his deputy and curtly motioned toward the spilled shotgun shells. "Fill your pockets!" he called over that outside hooting. "It's not them, Jack, it's the law. I already told you that."

Berryhill went over and wordlessly began scooping up shells. Duncan stepped away from that broken window, went to a bench, and dropped down watching the sheriff. Berryhill was nervous, but more than that he was obdurate. Clearly he did not like the position he now found himself in—what man would?—but he was no deviationist. If a battle started, he'd be in there with his riot gun, friends outside or enemies.

This should have made Duncan feel better but it didn't. He kept thinking what Berryhill had said about those men being his friends.

Jeremiah Parton glided away from that window, also, but he, from time to time, eyed the rack of upright Winchester carbines on across the room. Jack Thorne caught the bearded old man's calculating glance over there, and shook his head gently at Parton.

"You go ahead and try it if you want to," he said. "But when you do, remember one thing, old man . . . you'll be going for Big Casino. Either you make it good or you make it dead. Won't be any middle course at that distance if I line up your belly with this here scatter-gun."

Parton crossed over to where Duncan was sitting upright, alert to each discordant sound, eased down there, and glanced around at the younger man.

"They'll never get it done," he breathed, his rough tone full of conviction. "They can't no more

71

slip us out of here than they can fly. Listen to 'em out there."

"Pretty hard to hear anything else," Duncan commented, turning away from the old man.

Berryhill came over, looked first at Parton, then at Duncan as he leaned upon his shotgun, and said: "We could leave right now, only there's nothing but open country beyond town. They'd spot four riders before we were a mile out."

"Before we were ten feet out, you mean," corrected Parton. "You'd never get us past the door, Sheriff."

"The door be damned," said Berryhill. He got no chance to elaborate even if he'd intended to. All at once that roadway bedlam stopped as suddenly as though it had been turned off by a handle.

Berryhill sprang around but Jack Thorne was already moving toward the window ahead of him.

Thorne kept pressed to one side of the wall, craned his neck, and made one long, sweeping look out.

"What is it?" asked Berryhill.

"Over a dozen men with a batterin' ram, Matt. Have a look. The others are all gettin' back out of the way."

Thorne peered out again, longer this time because everyone out in the overflowing roadway was concentrating upon this oncoming log and its burly carriers.

"Dammit, Matt, I don't like this. Now we're goin' to have to shoot."

Duncan got up, watching the sheriff as he looked out, then stood rigidly for a long time before he started over toward the lawman.

Berryhill saw this from the corner of his eye and snarled: "Go back and sit down. And keep down."

Thorne protested again. "Matt, dammit. I don't want to fire into those fellows out there."

"Over their heads," retorted Berryhill. "Plenty high, Jack . . . just so they'll understand that we're not foolin'."

Thorne reluctantly poked his riot gun through the window, tilted its twin barrels, and fired off first one barrel, and then the other one. The roar of this weapon, plus the nearly total silence outside in the pre-dusk roadway, caused a sudden great commotion.

Every man out there, drunk or sober, knew that was a shotgun. Those carrying the log stood fast the longest, but when several of them cast loose to flee, the others could not continue forward so they ran, also.

Elsewhere that cannon-like roar scattered men like quail. They squawked and ran in every direction. A few drew six-guns and twisted to fire at the jailhouse as they fled, but not many. For some time there was only the solid beat of feet getting out of that exposed roadway. Later, guns were fired and within the jailhouse its occupants distinctly heard the patter of lead against brick.

Jack Thorne, standing well clear of the shattered window looked over at Matt Berryhill. "That did it!" he called over the increasing outside gunfire. "Now they're stirred up."

"They were anyway," retorted Sheriff Berryhill. He craned for an upward look at the mellowing sky. "Not much longer, Jack. Let 'em have a couple more high shots to keep 'em off."

Thorne obeyed but he did not expose himself. Bullets rained inside through that little window. He would wait for a lull, poke his scatter-gun out, tilt it, and fire it. Each time he did this, the others had to flatten against the front wall because slugs came through that window like leaden hail.

Old man Parton was the least collected man in Berryhill's office, and yet he was not so much afraid as he was apprehensive of the outcome of all this. Twice he asked Berryhill for permission to arm himself from that wall rack, and twice the sheriff swore at him.

Duncan, remembering that remark of Berryhill's about not using the door to leave, remained stationary with both shoulders pressed against the brick wall, watching Berryhill and considering what he might have meant.

The gunfire from outside had become sporadic. Sometimes it seemed to come in volley fashion. Other times it dwindled to only an occasional shot. Duncan noticed that neither the sheriff nor his deputy had much enthusiasm even for what little return shooting they did.

Parton edged over close and said to Duncan: "They're not half fightin'. It looks to me like them two are just puttin' up a mock defense."

"Berryhill has his reasons," muttered Duncan. "I'll stake my chances on him."

"Then you're a fool," Parton snarled, stepping away again.

Duncan swung to watch the old man. He was heading in the direction of that gun rack again. Both Berryhill and Thorne were occupied at the little window now, their backs facing the interior of the room.

Duncan hissed at Parton. The old man turned, glared, and started forward again, his intention obvious. Duncan stepped lightly away from his shielding wall, caught up with the old outlaw in four long strides, almost lazily lifted an arm, threw it out, caught Parton's shirt at the shoulder, and spun the older man around. Just as deliberate and slow-moving, Duncan's other arm came up. His balled fist caught Parton flush on the point of the jaw, dropping him like a pole-axed steer. That blow made its own sharp sound in the room.

Both Jack Thorne and the sheriff heard it, turned about, stepped clear of their little window, and swung their shotguns, held low.

Duncan looked over at them. For a moment

these three exchanged a stare. The outside gun-fire was swelling again so Duncan made no attempt to explain. He simply pointed to the rifle rack, to the sprawled bundle of old clothing and tough sinew at his feet, and shrugged his shoulders. Then he walked back over to his former position safely along the front wall.

Thorne and Berryhill exchanged a look. The sheriff spoke, Thorne nodded, and Berryhill swung away from him, approaching along the front wall toward Duncan. Thorne continued to man that wrecked window alone.

Berryhill paused to peer downward at Parton. The jailhouse was turning gloomy, dusk was settling, and one of those outside lulls added to the gloominess because it provided men with an opportunity to look about them at the wreckage they were responsible for.

"Hit him hard?" Berryhill asked with a mildly clinical interest. "Because if you did, one of us is going to have to carry him out of here, and that'll be quite a handicap."

"Hard enough," Duncan said.

Berryhill looked quickly up. "Why? Why didn't you let him get a gun?"

Duncan shook his head. "I'll probably die tonight, but I'm going to avoid it as long as I can. He'd have shot the three of us."

"Not you. Not his own son."

Duncan's anger flared. "I'm not his son, you

damned fool. He knows that and I know that. You and Thorne and a few others are the blind ones."

Berryhill looked down again. He shook his head wryly. He seemed on the verge of saying more, but Jack Thorne's soft call from over by the window interrupted.

"It's dark enough, Matt. We got to get out of here now."

Berryhill nodded. "Let's go," he said.

CHAPTER EIGHT

Duncan had no idea how Matt Berryhill proposed to get out of his jailhouse, and yet when he saw how the sheriff proposed to do this, it was so simple he was ashamed for not having anticipated something like it himself.

Berryhill went to his wall desk, grabbed the thing, and powerfully heaved it sideways. There, exposed for the first time, was a ring-bolted trap door. Berryhill bent, caught hold, lifted that squeaking old panel, eased it against the wall, and looked over where Duncan was watching.

"Pick him up," Berryhill ordered, motioning towards Jeremiah Parton, "and let's get out of here."

Duncan obeyed. Parton, for all his gaunt, tall height, did not weigh as much as Duncan thought he might. He hooked both arms under the old man, straightened up with him, and moved across the room.

"Easy now," cautioned Berryhill. "That old stairway hasn't been used in fifteen years."

Duncan shifted his grip, flinging Parton over one shoulder in order to have one hand free. Below him was total darkness and at his feet just below the trap door was a worn old stairway, leading down.

"What's down there?" he asked.

"That used to be where prisoners were kept in the early days. No one's used it for years. Don't worry, I'll be right behind you. Now go on."

Duncan stepped down, tested the first few steps, found them springy but not brittle, and descended into the clammy darkness, reaching out with his free hand for a wall that was not there.

This subterranean dungeon-like room was much larger than Duncan thought it would be. It had a graveyard odor to it and a clinging, chill kind of moldy air. He stepped away from the stairs, shifted Parton's weight a little, and groped off on his right until he eventually contacted an iron-bound cell door. Here he halted, turned about, and peered upward where the trap door's opening presented the only light at all. It was not enough actually to see much by because dusk was steadily moving in over the town.

Upstairs, Jack Thorne was still firing at intervals out the window but directly above Duncan, Sheriff Berryhill loomed up and began the descent. He no longer had his shotgun. He paused part way down, looked suspiciously into the lower darkness, and called out to Duncan.

"Light a match so I'll know where you are."

Duncan obeyed, manipulating this undertaking with one hand and mumbling: "This old devil's getting heavy. Get a move on, Sheriff."

Berryhill started down as soon as Duncan's

match flared. When he got to the bottom, he twisted and called out for Thorne to come along.

Duncan used his upheld match to view his surroundings. This underground place was surprisingly large and well made, but the moldy atmosphere was everywhere. Along the north wall, exactly as was the case upstairs in the jailhouse, there were individual cells. But these were not barred as were their counterparts overhead. They had been dug out of the solid ground and each one was faced with a massive, steel-wrapped oaken door. Every door had small, barred windows, not much larger than a man's hand.

Where Duncan stood, he could see a corridor ran southward beyond sight into the darkness. Then his match went out. He used both hands to shift old Parton to his other shoulder and flex his arms. When Berryhill struck a match, Duncan looked upward.

Jack Thorne was standing at the top of the stairs looking larger than life in the sooty gloom. Berryhill told Thorne to leave his shotgun behind. Duncan heard Thorne toss the weapon aside and start down. He paused once, bent far out, caught the trap door, and lowered it over his descending head. Now, except for Berryhill's upheld match, the darkness jumped out all around, forming a solid wall.

Old Parton groaned and Jack Thorne, just stepping off the stairway, whipped around straining to see. Duncan tightened his hold around the old man's dangling legs and Berryhill explained to Thorne what the noise was.

The three of them started off southward with Sheriff Berryhill in the lead, lighting matches along the way. He hiked along as only a man could in this dark place who knew every foot of the ground he was traversing. From time to time they halted when a match went out, but otherwise their progress was steady and swift.

Duncan was surprised at the length of the corridor Berryhill led them through. He thought it ran well out under the jailhouse proper and under some adjoining buildings. Then it abruptly cut north, narrowed, and the last time Berryhill struck a fresh match, in that first flaring brilliance Duncan saw another stairway.

Berryhill started up gingerly, testing these old steps as each of them had tested those by the jailhouse entry. Duncan was still at the bottom when Berryhill put out his match, raised both burly arms, and strained mightily. A trap door opened with protest on ancient and rusty springs. Hay and chaff and fresh night air came downward. Berryhill disappeared beyond that opening, and when Duncan would have pushed upward, Thorne growled at him to wait.

The sheriff returned, jerked upward with his thumb, and helped each of his companions, in turn, up out of the ground.

Parton began to move weakly, move his feet a little, and mutter. Duncan stepped clear of the black hole behind him, eased over, and slid the old man off his shoulder. A sensation of weight-lessness immediately made Duncan feel almost airborne. He rolled his shoulders and moved his arms to restore full circulation.

They were in a barn. As near as Duncan could tell it had to be one of the barns across the alley from the jailhouse. Berryhill faded out some-where in the building with only the soft fall of his footsteps audible over the dry hay. When Duncan craned around, Jack Thorne was there looking at old Parton.

"Gone for the horses," Thorne murmured, speaking of the lawman. "You sure belted this old gaffer."

Duncan bent, caught Parton's shoulder, and effortlessly hoisted the old outlaw to his feet. He gently shook him.

"Come on," he said quietly. "Come out of it, you old devil. You're not hurt."

It was too gloomy to make out Parton's expression, but both of them watched him put up an arm and move his hand to explore his bearded jaw very gingerly. He stood unsteadily peering from Duncan to Thorne and back again to Duncan.

"What happened?" he hoarsely asked. "Where am I?"

"Safe," muttered Jack Thorne. "A damned sight safer you got any right to expect to be. What happened? Why, your boy here just cracked you on the jaw is all."

Duncan swung, caught burly Jack Thorne by the shirt, and drew the older, thicker man to him. "Gun or no gun!" he exclaimed. "You call me this old devil's son once more and I'll whittle you down to size." He flung Thorne away from him, his face a pale, wrathful blur.

Thorne acted more astonished than angry. He took one more backward step and he kept staring in a puzzled way, but he said nothing until Berryhill returned leading four saddled horses. Two of those animals had jutting Winchester stocks nearly straight up by the saddle swells. He tossed one set of reins to Thorne, kept one set, and jerked with his head for Duncan and Parton to claim the other two animals.

"It's plenty dark outside," he said, speaking crisply. "They're still shooting around on Main Street, so we just might make it." He looked straight at Duncan and old Parton. "One word of warning . . . when we ride out of here, you two stay real close to Jack and me. One funny move and you get dropped in your tracks, and if either of us shoots, that mob of cowboys around there will figure out what's happening, get astride, and be after us like a herd of Apaches, so even if Jack or I miss, you'll still get run down and lynched."

Berryhill nodded for Thorne to mount up first, then stood there until Jack was across leather with his six-gun fisted, before he mounted himself. "Stay behind 'em," he said to Thorne. "All right you two . . . mount up."

Duncan could only very faintly hear that continuing gunfire easterly until Berryhill opened one side of a large set of double doors. After that night air rushed in, bringing with it the full thunder of all those guns. He looked around at old Parton who fell into line behind him, saw the old man's glittering eyes and wild beard, saw Jack Thorne behind Parton, then swung forward, and eased out his horse behind Sheriff Berryhill.

They left the barn in a walk. In fact, they made no attempt to hasten until they were well clear of Leesville's westernmost scattered houses, and even then Berryhill, who set the pace, only loped out, he did not run his animal.

For several hundred yards they rode like this— Berryhill out front, carbine cradled over his lap, loping gently westerly, behind him Duncan, then Parton, and finally burly Jack Thorne. Not a word was said. Each man was alert to deadly peril and constantly raked the star-bright night for movement, for shadows, for anything that might mean danger.

A mile beyond town Berryhill halted, shifted around, and stared over their back trail. Still none of them spoke. The night was softly lit all around them, but visibility did not exceed a hundred yards in any direction.

Duncan saw the sheriff's thick shoulders turn loose and slump a little. Jack Thorne, riding with one hand on that projecting Winchester butt, dropped both hands to the saddle horn.

"Made it," he succinctly said. "Don't mind saying, though, I got more gray hairs now than I had three, four hours ago." He saw Duncan watching him, started to make a wry little smile, checked himself in this, and looked away from Duncan over to Sheriff Berryhill. "Nice night, Matt," he murmured with elaborate unconcern.

Berryhill's deep set eyes shone ironically. "Beautiful, Jack," he murmured back. "Now all we got to do is steer clear of riders, head due west over the county line, and deposit our friends here in the jailhouse over at Bradley."

Parton spoke for the first time since they'd left Leesville. He looked less apprehensive now and more perplexed. "Tell me, boys," he asked. "Just how in hell did we get out of that lousy jailhouse and over into that cussed barn?"

Duncan saw Berryhill's twinkle deepen as the sheriff replied to this. "It's an old Indian disappearin' trick," he said. "You close your eyes, open your mouth real wide, Parton. Take a big breath and jump down your own throat. It turns you inside out and you become invisible. That's what we did, then we just plain walked out."

Berryhill lifted the reins, turned, and started riding again.

Down the line Parton swore under his breath at the sheriff and continued to mutter bleakly to himself for almost a full mile farther along before Duncan, wearying of the language, said: "Shut up, Parton."

The old man shut up.

Eventually they could no longer hear gunshots faintly popping behind them. Duncan was not sure that this was entirely due to the widening distance. He thought it was just as possible that those men back there had gotten into the jailhouse and found it empty. For a while after that he rode with his head turned the slightest bit, but after a while, with no running horses to be detected in the surrounding night, Duncan relaxed, looped his reins, fished for his tobacco sack, and worked up a cigarette. When he lit up, he did so behind the shielding brim of his hat. After that he passed along feeling almost jaunty, feeling as though his lease on life had just been renewed.

Once Berryhill stopped, dismounted, pressed his ear to the ground, remained in that position for quite a while, then got back upright.

"Anything?" asked Thorne.

Berryhill shook his head. "Thought I heard something northward and a little onward, but it was probably just some cattle. Nothing from behind us, though."

They went on again as far as a stone trough. Here, they halted to water the animals and stretch their legs.

Here, Duncan asked Berryhill how far this next town of Bradley was.

"Ought to be there by midday tomorrow," answered the lawman. "You got any more of that tobacco?" Duncan passed over the makings. Jack Thorne also stepped up to make a smoke.

As Berryhill passed over the sack and papers, he said to Duncan: "You know, when you're around men, you sort of get the hang of how their minds work." Berryhill lit up, stared straight at Duncan over the match's quick flare, shook his head, and dropped the match when it winked out. "I can't quite figure you out. Some way or another you just don't fit the part. Your paw does . . . he fits it to a T, but not you. It puzzles me."

Thorne also lit up. He snapped his match and said: "Matt, you better not call old Parton his paw. He came within an ace of sluggin' me back under the jailhouse for sayin' that."

Thorne drawled this, his head up and his thoughtful, skeptical gaze full on Duncan. Old Parton, off to one side of the other three, gradually bent, turning stiff while listening. The others did not observe this. In fact, they paid the old man no attention at all.

Berryhill dropped his gaze, carefully inspected

his cigarette's glowing tip, and shrugged. "We'll get it all sorted out one of these days. There's something here I don't quite understand yet." He raised his eyes. "Well, let's get riding. From here on there's just a lot of range country to get across. I think the worst is behind us."

They mounted. The last man up was old Parton, and if they'd heeded him, they would have noticed the puzzled expression the old man wore, but none of them more than casually glanced at him.

Thorne pushed back his hat, deeply inhaled, deeply exhaled, and said to no one in particular: "You don't have to be soft in the brain to wear one of these badges, but it sure helps. Those boys back there are goin' to be raggin' me for the next five years about lettin' myself get deputized tonight, then sneakin' away like this."

"Somebody had to do it," said Berryhill. "You know that and so do they, Jack."

"Yeah, I expect so."

Duncan kept still. He did not know the country they were traveling across, but he recognized some of those watery mountain peaks off on his right, having come down that way into this country two days earlier.

Duncan wagged his head. This had been the wildest two days he'd ever lived through. They didn't seem like two days; they seemed like two years. He finished his smoke, broke it on his saddle horn, and dropped it. He looked ahead at Berryhill, looked back at Jack Thorne, looked last at old Jeremiah Parton directly behind him. He looked longest at the older man, too, because Parton, for some inexplicable reason was riding back there smiling.

CHAPTER NINE

Two things began annoying Duncan after another hour of pacing slowly down this bland, quiet night—hunger and weariness.

His last meal had been shortly before high noon and it now was, by his estimate, close to 11:00 p.m. As for rest—he hadn't had any since the day before he'd been picked up by Berryhill's posse at the cottonwood spring. He'd tried to rest the previous night but that had been a dismal failure.

Still, even after boredom came to increase his weariness and he had had time to dwell upon his empty stomach, he could accept these discomforts philosophically. After all, he was alive, and that was more than he'd expected to be by this time since the sun had come into his jail cell this same morning.

But old Parton began nagging for food and rest in his usual raffish, grating tone, as soon as all four of them were passing along drowsily without a thought of danger in any of their minds. He complained, too, about having to keep up this steady riding.

Duncan, listening to this whining, shook his head wryly. Parton had already forgotten how frightened he'd been back in the Leesville jailhouse when he had been certain that he was going to be lynched. Duncan's contempt for the old bearded outlaw grew until, when he could stand no more of that bitter complaining, he said: "Parton, if you don't close your mouth and keep it closed, I'm going to step down and drag you off that horse and gag you."

"If," came back the old man's shrewish reply, "I had a gun, boy, you'd be talkin' out the other side of your face for that remark."

"Sure," said Duncan. "Sure. But I'd have to turn my back on you first."

Berryhill slowed, let Duncan come even with him, then he said: "Tell me something . . . why didn't you just throw down on that traveler instead of shooting him to get his gun and shell belt?"

Duncan's weariness made him heave a big sigh over this. "Your skull's solid stone," he told Berryhill. "*I* didn't kill that man!"

Berryhill looked tart. "You just found his gun belt floatin' around in the air," he said.

"That was *my* gun and shell belt, Sheriff. *Mine* . . . m-i-n-e. If you want to find the belt off that dead man, pick up that trail you were following when you came upon the dead stranger, ride it down to its ending, and you'll not only find the dead man's gun, you'll also find the fellow who shot him for it . . . old Parton's son."

Berryhill rode along another few feet, staring

over at Duncan, wagged his head, and reined back to ride stirrup with Jack Thorne.

This was the way they were moving along when the land turned gradually rough and eroded with occasional stone spires jutting against the over-head star-speckled heavens.

Somewhere deep and far out in this wilder country a panther screamed, and, closer, startled deer or antelope rattled over stones in panic at the sound and scent of ridden horses passing through. They bounded away in a frantic rush bringing to Duncan's mind the agreeable thought of venison steaks.

They were parallel now with those upthrusts that Duncan had passed around to come down into this country. Dead ahead, due west, he could faintly make out another southward-curving spur of those same hills. Somewhere ahead there would be another pass, this one leading into new land and eventually to a town named Bradley. He was not interested in the town, but he passed the silent time by trying to guess, from land forms, just how much farther they would have to ride.

Old Parton, drifting along off to Duncan's left, was constantly swinging his head. Duncan thought he was doing this to keep awake. He had no idea the old man had caught sounds moving ahead of them, back at that stone trough. Neither did Berryhill nor Thorne, who were bringing up the rear, desultorily talking back and forth, until, without any warning whatsoever, and catching every one of those four men totally unprepared, a black-clad figure rose up almost under the hoofs of Duncan's mount causing the beast to lurch back, stiffen its front legs, and come to an abrupt, faintly snorting halt.

That blurry onward figure, with its back to a mighty stone spire, was exceedingly difficult to separate from the surrounding night, but one thing was not at all difficult to discern—a Winchester carbine glistened in faint star shine pointing straight at those four bunched-up horsemen.

Sheriff Berryhill and his deputy were caught with both hands lying idle upon their saddle horns. For the space of a long pent-up breath none of the horsemen moved. Even their animals seemed suddenly turned to stone.

"You there," came a muffled voice, indicating Duncan who was foremost, "get down and lead your horse off to the left."

Duncan did not move.

A gloved thumb cocked that Winchester, and Berryhill said quietly: "Do as he says . . . get down and walk off to the left."

Duncan swung out and down, led his mount away, and halted to watch what must now ensue. He tried to determine whether or not that black wraith was alone, but could not. It was too dark over there by that thick spire to see anything but that cocked saddle gun.

"The rest of you . . . ride on."

Sheriff Berryhill started to say something, perhaps to protest, but he never got to complete even his initial sentence. That muffled voice snarled an order and emphasized it with a curt swing of the carbine.

"I said ride on!"

Thorne picked up his reins, sighed, shook his head at Berryhill, and growled at old Parton, who sat his horse looking completely speechless, with his bearded lips parted.

"Go on, Parton . . . do like he says. Move out!"

Duncan watched the others ride off. He was certain now that he could detect at least two people over in among the boulders, but he remained with his intention fixed upon that tall, black-attired rider with the Winchester.

It did not seem possible to him that, whatever the purpose behind all this was, he had been selected at random from among his four former companions, and yet he was totally at a loss to understand why he had been cut out of that little riding band.

The Winchester swung. "Mount up!" its owner ordered Duncan. "Ride at a walk over here."

Duncan turned, toed in, and stepped up. He could not now discern those former companions of his at all, out in the night. It occurred to him that they would be halting out there somewhere, perhaps even creeping back. He thought at least

Matt Berryhill would try this because he had the sheriff pegged as a stubborn man unlikely to take the loss of a prisoner without a struggle.

When he got over to the dark spire, two riders were waiting there, one tall, one short and appearing frail. Without a word the taller one gestured with the carbine for Duncan to ride ahead.

"North," he said, "and lope. Don't try to run, just lope. Head out."

Duncan tried mightily to see that rider's face, failed again, reined out, lightly roweled his mount, and went rocketing northward through the hushed and balmy night.

For an hour Duncan led the other two, until the one with the carbine gestured easterly. Duncan obediently eased off in that direction and another hour passed before the trio of them came to more broken country. Here, with the backdrop mountains close enough to cast their darker shadows over the flat country for a considerable distance, the rifle-bearing rider dressed all in black called a halt.

"Get down!"

Duncan alighted. It was beginning to annoy him the way those sharp orders were given. Still, at least for the time being, there was nothing he could do about that. "Lead your horse and head for that first arroyo ahead of you."

Once more Duncan led out, this time on foot.

His temper was steadily rising. Whoever those two behind him were, they seemed to know this wild foothill country. Or at least the one with the carbine seemed to know it. He couldn't see much of the other rider.

A wide dip appeared leading down into a deep, wide erosion gulch. Duncan hiked down here, suspecting the reason for their doing this was to prevent Berryhill—should he follow this far—from being able to skyline them against the paler eastern sky.

He was correct. As soon as his captors came down into the arroyo, they both dismounted, attempting to go no farther.

Duncan turned for a closer look but was thwarted again. Down in this place it was pitch dark, almost as totally black as it had been back in Leesville under the jailhouse.

The frailer, less active of his captors took their three horses, walked on up the arroyo a little distance, and tied them there. He came back afterward, and meanwhile the other one stood across from Duncan with that Winchester cradled, staring over at his prisoner, saying nothing nor moving.

When the two were together again, the taller one said in that same muffled way: "All right. Let's have the truth about you. What's your name?"

"Duncan. Todd Duncan. And if you think I had a hand in killing that . . ."

"Be quiet! You answer. I'll do the asking. Where are you from?"

"Montana."

"Where were you going when you came into this country?"

"Well, no place exactly. I sort of had an idea of getting a riding job down here some place . . . Arizona, New Mexico . . . some place where the winters are milder than they are in Montana."

"What's your name?"

"I already told you."

"Tell us again."

"Todd Duncan . . . dammit."

"Matthew Berryhill said you killed that stranger lying at the embalming shed back in town just to steal his guns and shell belt."

Duncan's anger was bubbling. "What the hell," he said roughly. "I haven't killed anyone. I just came riding through, is all."

"Can you prove any of this?"

"Prove? What is there to prove? Look, mister whoever-you-are, if you folks hereabouts are convinced I committed these here crimes, it's up to you to prove that I did. It's not up to me to prove I didn't commit 'em."

That tall, slender gunman said something now that made Duncan's jaw sag. "We know you didn't kill that stranger. What we don't know is whether or not you are the one who shot Mister Dudley in the express office."

Duncan stared for a moment, felt behind him for an earthen barranca, and leaned upon it. "How do you know I didn't kill that traveler?" he asked.

"Easy. The doctor in town told us you couldn't have killed him. He was gunned down at the time when, according to our figures, you were in jail."

Duncan ran this through his mind. He reached up, eased his hat back, and said: "I didn't think of that."

"Neither did Matthew Berryhill or Jack Thorne, evidently."

"Is that why you took me away from there . . . to get at the truth?"

"Partly that, yes. Partly because we feel that where there has been one bad error, it's possible there might also be another."

Duncan's long-dead hope revived. "You're not going to hang me?"

"No."

"Then tell me something, mister . . . just who the hell are you and what's your interest in all this?"

"My interest is elemental. I want the truth about that murder of Charles Dudley. I think you have the key to that, and I don't want you hanged until I get it. The whole truth."

"Mister," Duncan said, speaking rapidly, "all I can tell you about that, is that when I found

Swindin out there on the southward desert, it was the first time I'd ever laid eyes on him. Sure, I made supper for the two of us . . . but I thought he was asleep over against that damned tree. Listen, do you think, if I'd known Swindin was dead, I'd have laid out two plates and two cups? Of course not. Neither would you. The next thing I knew Berryhill, Thorne, and some other men had the drop on me from behind. They brought me to Leesville and you probably know the rest of it . . . I was tossed into jail, a lynch mob formed, and Berryhill got all of us out of it. From there on it's your party . . . you took me away from Berryhill."

When Duncan ceased speaking, those two exchanged a look. The shorter one nodded, shuffled forward where star shine struck his face. He tilted back his hat so that Duncan could see him clearly.

It was the elderly priest.

The second one stepped forward, removed the black hat, shook out a tumble of taffy-blonde hair, and Duncan gasped. It was Marianne Dudley.

CHAPTER TEN

The dead expressman's daughter gave Duncan very little chance to evidence his astonishment at finding she was the one who had held up Sheriff Berryhill with a rifle.

"There was something else that made us feel you were likely to be hanged before your degree of guilt had been established, Mister Duncan," she said, standing there tall and slim in her man's attire. "Father Peter followed the trail of Sheriff Berryhill and Jack Thorne yesterday."

"All right," said Duncan. "What did that prove?"

"They turned back when they met the man who'd found that dead stranger. Father Peter didn't . . . he kept on following that trail." Marianne turned, held out her hand, and the priest placed a rumpled cloth in it. She held this out for Duncan to take. He took the thing, held it up, and peered closely at it.

"This thing is stiff with . . ." Duncan broke off, understanding coming.

Marianne finished the sentence for him.

"Blood. Father Peter found that at a water hole up here in the foothills. He also found a camp where one man had rested for what he thought must have been nearly half a day."

"Parton's son," breathed Duncan. He swung

toward the elderly priest. "Did you find him? I mean did you stay on his trail?"

Father Peter shook his head. "I'm afraid it was much too rough a trail for a man of my years, Mister Duncan. But now you'll understand why Miss Marianne and I decided we could not stand idly by and see you hanged."

Duncan looked from one of them to the other. An old man and a beautiful girl—what an unlikely pair of allies to prevent a man from being hanged. He went for his tobacco sack, dropped his head, and fashioned a smoke. When he lit up and exhaled, Marianne was holding something out toward him. A blue steel six-gun. He looked above this weapon into the girl's face.

"You got a little too much trust in you," he murmured, and took the gun, checked it, found it completely loaded, and pushed it into his waistband. "You could be wrong, you know. I could be something a lot different than you think I am."

She shook her head gently at him. "You couldn't be as different as Matt and Jack think you are."

For a moment those two stood there considering each other. She was, in her man's black shirt and trousers, compellingly desirable, with her full blouse and long legs, and her steady, dead-level eyes.

"Tell me something," Duncan said, watching her face closely. "Why didn't you just take this old bandage to Berryhill?"

It was the priest who answered this. "We couldn't, Mister Duncan. I didn't get back to town until late last night and I was too tired." Father Peter lifted his shoulders and let them drop. "We had no idea that talk would erupt into actual mob violence today, so I went home and retired with the intention of seeing Sheriff Berryhill this afternoon. Well, you can imagine the rest of it. When Marianne and I got together this afternoon, Sheriff Berryhill was barricaded in his jailhouse and no one could get in to talk to him."

"One more question. How did you two manage to get around Berryhill's party out here and manage to waylay it?"

"That wasn't difficult," spoke up Marianne. "But we weren't certain which way he would try to escape town after he used the old-time underground passageway out of his jailhouse. So, we saddled up, rode out a little ways from his barn, and simply sat there, waiting. When we saw the four of you ride out, we waited to make certain you would go west, then we tried to keep well north of you and parallel . . . which we did . . . until we were sure you wouldn't change course, then all we had to do was get into the rocks and waylay you."

"Yeah," muttered Duncan. "That's all you had to do. Don't you know how close you were to being killed, girl? Why, hell's bells, if either Berryhill or Thorne had happened to have their right hands free, they'd have gone for their guns."

"That's why we dressed in black, Mister Duncan. That's also why we chose the backdrop we used." Marianne paused, then said in a fatalistic way: "There had to be some risks taken."

"No, ma'am, you could have walked out and handed Berryhill that bandage. You didn't have to abduct me at gunpoint."

"Are you sorry that we did, Mister Duncan?"

"Well . . . no. But . . ."

"But you'd prefer having men more like yourself with you when you go after my father's murderer, is that it?"

Duncan squirmed. "Don't think I don't appreciate what you're doing, ma'am. But it's likely to be a long trail and a rough one. Remember, wounded or not, young Parton's got a long lead. The trail will be hard and probably long, and at the end of it there could be death for someone. Now that just isn't the environment for a pretty girl and a priest, you got to admit that."

Marianne looked around at Father Peter. "I can't agree with that, can you?"

The priest ran a blue-veined hand over his jaw. He considered Marianne and he considered lank, powerful Todd Duncan, also. Somewhere here, he thought, he'd been passed by. There was something yeasty springing to life between those two.

"Well," he said dubiously, "Marianne, at my age a long trail and considerable hardship does not exactly tempt me. Yet on the other hand, I think Mister Duncan is not entirely correct, either. You see, young man, that was Marianne's father who was murdered. Wouldn't you say she was entitled to take an active part in finding his killer?"

Duncan inhaled deeply off his cigarette, exhaled deeply, dropped the thing, and stepped upon it. "Father," he stated in an exasperated, rough voice, "there likely will be shooting. There's no way of telling where this trail might go. Now what right has a nice girl got to be traipsing around in a situation like that?"

The priest, from the corner of his eye, saw Marianne stiffen, draw up erect, and shoot her flashing stare across at Duncan.

He said quickly: "Mister Duncan, although I somewhat agree with you, I think, too, you should remember that Marianne is not entirely incapable of handling firearms, and that except for her, you would not be in a position to demonstrate your innocence of the murder charge against you. Now then . . . under those circumstances, don't you think she's entitled to make up her own mind?"

"You mean make her own mistakes," Duncan growled, and glared. He turned and said: "Miss Marianne, please . . . you've done a right smart job of freeing me and I really appreciate that, but won't you just go on back and tend to your knitting, or whatever you got to do back home in Leesville?"

"No! If you're going after young Parton, I'm going with you. He killed my father."

Duncan, seeing the obdurate set of her jaw, the tough set of her stance across from him in the soft star shine, recognized the futility of additional argument. He ruefully bobbed his head up and down.

"All right, ma'am," he said.

Marianne did not look away from Duncan. She said: "Father, you can put the saddlebags behind my saddle now, if you will." At Duncan's mild look of inquiry she said: "Food and extra ammunition, Mister Duncan. Parton's trail leads straight up into these northward hills and there are no more towns or ranches once we ride north out of this arroyo."

Duncan said dryly: "I know. I just came over that north country." He pursed his lips, studied Marianne a moment, then added: "You had it all planned, didn't you?"

"Yes."

"And supposing you'd failed?"

She let that defiant expression soften a little toward him. "I didn't plan on failing, Mister Duncan. You see, I know Matthew Berryhill and Jack Thorne. They are good men, but what I needed for this job was a tough man. You were the only one around, so I planned not to fail just as I also planned to free you and accompany you."

"You could've been shot, you know."

"Mister Duncan . . . there are worse things than dying."

He stood there assessing her for a while, then he smiled. "You're quite a woman, Marianne. I don't know as I ever before met one like you."

She did not return his smile nor acknowledge his sincere compliment. She simply turned, walked to her horse, thrust the Winchester into its saddle boot, watched Father Peter finish lashing the saddlebags aft of her cantle, then she swung up. She and the old priest exchanged a long, warm look. He smiled and she impulsively put a hand down to him.

"You'll tell Sheriff Berryhill, Father?"

"Aye. As soon as the both of us get back to Leesville." Father Peter's smile dwindled a little as an unpleasant thought occurred to him. "He's not going to like it at all, Marianne . . . but we knew that, didn't we?"

She squeezed his hand and nodded.

Father Peter stepped back until she'd reined around to face Duncan. He said: "Good luck, the both of you." Then stood there as he watched them silently ride up northward out of the arroyo.

Upon the overhead lip of land Duncan halted to look back and see that the old priest got astride his animal without difficulty.

Father Peter gathered his reins and threw Duncan a casual wave as he turned his beast toward the upward and southward trail.

Without taking his eyes off Father Peter, Duncan said to Marianne: "He's quite a man . . . quite a man."

"You don't know him, Mister Duncan, so you have no idea of just how right you are. He's one of the finest men you'll ever know."

Duncan did not attempt to push on, instead he swung, studied the beautiful girl wryly, and said: "Let's get a couple of things straight right now. First off . . . I make the decisions and give the orders. Next . . . my name is Todd and your name is Marianne."

"All right."

"All right, what?"

"All right, Todd."

Duncan lifted his reins and started forward toward the battlemented mountains dead ahead. After a while he said: "Do you know this country up in here?"

"Yes, I've been riding these hills since I was a little girl."

"Have you any idea where young Parton might have gone, up here?"

"Father Peter followed his tracks as far as Bear Springs. That's a meadow on ahead of us about two miles. After that, I'm afraid we'll have to await daylight to track him farther."

"Ride on ahead," directed Duncan. "Make for this Bear Springs, and I'll follow you."

Marianne dutifully passed around Duncan,

struck out in an angling, easterly way and almost at once passed out of the prairie's pale light into forest gloom. She cut back and forth until she came upon a game trail, and afterward she did not leave this trail.

The forest was dark and fragrant. It was also carpeted with a spongy, ageless turf upon which their mounts did not make a sound. Once, they startled a fat brown bear out of his bed, and as he went crashing away down the hillside some aroused birds in the overhead treetops drowsily complained about this interruption of their slumber.

Duncan watched Marianne ride. She was lithe and shapely up there on her saddle and she handled her mount as only experienced riders can. She did not now seem at all like a town girl, and this set him to wondering about her. When she'd visited him at the jailhouse, she'd been attired in a dress. She'd seemed then entirely citified and feminine.

He decided, before this hunt was over, he would find out more about her, more about her dead father, too.

It was pleasant riding up in this forest with her, so pleasant he almost forgot why he was up in here. Almost forgot, too, that somewhere out on the plain below a furious sheriff and his burly deputy would be cursing a blue streak over his abduction and escape.

CHAPTER ELEVEN

They got to Bear Springs after midnight. Under a failing moon it was difficult to examine the ground but Duncan found all he had to see to know that Jeremiah Parton's son had been gone from this place at least one full day.

Here, he and Marianne had an argument. She was for remaining at the springs and he was for pushing on. She reminded him of what he'd said back in the arroyo, but he argued that this was no longer pertinent, that what they must do now was steal a march upon her father's slayer.

"If he hasn't gotten over the rims, we might be ambushed!" she exclaimed.

"Listen . . . that man is wounded and he'll be dog-tired from all his riding and hiding. I expect he'll be sleeping like a log on ahead somewhere."

"He'd hear us nonetheless, or his horse would."

"Not on these pine needles he wouldn't."

"Well," said Marianne, her temper up. "You go ahead if you wish, but I'm staying here until sunup."

Duncan stood up. "I don't know the way or I would," he snapped.

"There are game trails. They lead on around the slope and over the top out. It's a long way and it's hard riding. My guess is that despite his lead, he'll be on this side of the rimrocks."

"Your guess," snorted Duncan. "You get up onto that horse and lead out, or I'll put you up there. I told you back on the range, I'd make the decisions and give the orders. You agreed to that. Now I'm telling you . . . get on that horse!"

Marianne whirled and glared. "You wouldn't dare," she said.

Duncan teetered where he stood, restrained by inhibitions from laying a hand on her, and, as moments passed, sorry he'd said that because it put him in a position where, if she didn't obey him, he would have to back up his words with action, or ignominiously back down. And Todd Duncan wasn't the backing-down kind.

They stood less than twenty feet apart with the little spring and its scuffed ground between them.

He tried temporizing and softened his voice to her. "Marianne, you point the way and I'll ride well ahead, so if there's shooting, you'll be plumb out of it. But try to understand . . . Berryhill will pick up my trail come daylight. He'll be in these hills by noon. Whatever we do, we've got to do now."

"Berryhill couldn't find us in here. Not if we knew he was trying to. Dawn will help us go directly to my father's killer. Besides, these animals need a rest."

"They can rest after we find Parton," Duncan

110

said, his control slipping. "We've wasted enough time. Get on that horse."

"No!"

He looked at her. He dropped his reins and took a reluctant step forward, his face grim as though he were going into battle.

She saw his expression and said quickly, almost in horror: "No! Don't you dare try!"

He kept on walking.

She reached for one of her split reins, doubled it, and raised it. "If you touch me, you'll wish you hadn't, Todd Duncan."

He stopped with two feet separating them. She stood there ready to lash out at him with that upraised leather strap.

"Don't make me do it this way," he said.

They stood glaringly adamant, both of them breathing hard. Both of them stubbornly dogged in their resolve. Their eyes locked and their bodies tense.

Marianne abruptly turned, toed in, and sprang up over leather, refusing to look down at him and becoming very occupied in adjusting her reins with meticulous attention.

He did not say a word. He went back to his own animal, mounted it, and swung away from Bear Springs. At the clearing's edge where thick forest closed down again with its powerful darkness he twisted to gaze at her.

"This same trail?" he asked.

"Yes. Keep going until I tell you differently."

He settled back around and kneed out his horse. There was a dim paleness where the trail went crookedly in and out among immense red-barked pines. There were interminable little feeder trails coming into this main trail, but it was not difficult even in the weak light of early morning to determine which was the main trail and which was not.

After an hour's riding Duncan halted, got down, and paced ahead with a match flare to make certain they were not following just a trail. They weren't. The tracks of a shod horse lay there plainly evident in six inches of ancient dust. He got back astride, said nothing to Marianne, and struck out again.

This main trail went easterly around the mountainside until a granite switch-back was encountered, then it twisted back upon itself at a higher altitude and went westerly again. In this manner it see-sawed back and forth always climbing, but never so steep it could not be easily navigated. It was an ancient thoroughfare, and where it crossed bare rock, it was cut a foot deep indicating that men and animals had used it for hundreds of years.

Those lesser trails that came into it here and there rose up out of cañons as though they had been made by animals seeking water and returning from this quest to pass along again over the central trail way. There was an occasional windfall pine or fir tree to be skirted, and once a recently tumbled small tree had to be jumped. But generally this was a good trail.

It wound around a brushy knoll, then broke out, when Duncan least expected it, into a water grass meadow. Here, after passing a sentinel pine of great girth and age, lay a little fry-pan lake. And here, too, they startled a band of night-feeding elk that fled from them, but without any panic.

"From here on," Marianne said, "there are alternating marshes and meadows. He could be at any one of them."

Duncan bobbed his head up and down. "How far before these meadows peter out and we're back on that mountainside again?"

"About two miles, I'd guess. There's a fine big meadow ahead about a mile from this little skillet lake."

"He may be there," Duncan said, and kept on riding even though his horse would have stopped.

"If he isn't," retorted Marianne, "he'll have made it over the rimrocks and down the other side."

Duncan stayed on the trail. He rode easily in the saddle but vigilant. He did not believe young Parton would be lying along here any place for the elemental reason that any seasoned Westerner would know, from the widening, broadening land forms roundabout, there would be an even larger, more lush, and well watered meadow on ahead through the last fringe of trees.

Marianne, though, had her misgivings. Twice she murmured warnings and twice Duncan ignored them as he slouched along watching the trees press in, then drop back again, always becoming thinner in their stands, less grim and forbidding in their grouped darkness.

The trail dropped down, crossed a brawling little white-water creek, went up a dusty trail through another spit of pines, then, where those trees fell away again, going east and west on around, there lay a large meadow with a lake at its far end. Stars were in that lake; the water was like glass. Behind it rose up a solid, rough rock wall upon whose towering heights stood some ragged old bull pines looking for all the world like dejected, vanquished giants, against the paling easterly sky.

"If he hasn't gone on by now," Duncan said, drawing rein in the last tree fringe so Marianne could come up even with him, "he'll be some-where hereabouts."

Marianne said nothing as she ran a slow, careful look ahead.

Duncan swung down, handed up his reins, and said: "Stay here and don't make any noise. I'll see if I can locate his horse."

He went twistingly in among the trees south-ward until he was shielded, then he began passing carefully around this large emerald meadow with its twenty-acre lake and its great depth of solitude, moving as an Indian would have moved. He would go ahead fifty or a hundred feet, then halt to test the area roundabout where he stood motionlessly. Moving each time from shadow to shadow, from tree to tree.

In this manner he got within sight of an old tumble-down line rider's log cabin and here he saw what he was seeking. A grazing horse was moving drowsily from one hummock of tufted grass to another.

Duncan got as close as he dared to this animal, saw caked sweat stains, glided on nearer to the cabin, saw a saddle with the blanket and bridle hanging from a tree where porcupines could not get at it, and paused to check the gun Marianne had given him.

The horse threw up its head, swung around, and sniffed the little vagrant breeze coming on from the direction of Marianne and their own horses, and whinnied.

Duncan froze.

For a long time there was no reaction to this obvious call of one horse to another horse, but from within the shack came the unmistakable rattle of spur rowels. Duncan swore fiercely to himself. The horse had awakened his owner and there was only one way to approach that cabin because, excepting the north wall, there was neither a door nor a window, and approaching it now across a grassy star-lit meadow would be an invitation for the man in there to shoot him.

He debated whether or not to go back for Marianne and their animals. He thought, if he allowed that unseen man to rest easy for a little while, his vigilance might slacken. He also thought that if that man should get out of the cabin, without Duncan seeing him, and find Marianne with their two horses, he could very easily put Duncan afoot in these mountains, which would be a prime disaster.

Duncan went back the way he'd come, found Marianne standing with their animals, her Winchester cradled but ready, and explained to her what he'd found. She seemed not the least surprised.

"I'm familiar with that cabin," she told Duncan. "The cowmen use it when their cattle are ranging the mountains during the summer. It was built by trappers about fifty years ago."

"Well," growled Duncan, "they built it to stand off Indians from the looks of it. There's only one way in and one way out." He paused to look at her a thoughtful moment. "I'll trade you guns," he said, holding out the six-gun. "If we can't surprise him in there, this will turn into a rifle duel because the range is too great for six-guns."

She dutifully handed over the Winchester, took his six-gun, and waited for his next directive.

"We'll lead our horses around through the trees

and you'll stay with them. If he gets out and runs off our stock . . ."

"I understand," she calmly said. "Lead out."

He went back the way he'd come but slower this time because the horses had to be watched lest they scent that grazing animal and call to it.

The sky was steadily paling now, up where those forlorn old bull pines stood watch atop their dizzying heights. There was a clean scent to this pre-dawn time of day, a definite fragrance of virgin country, but for now Duncan ignored everything but the excitement he felt at nearing the end of the trail.

Up ahead in the cabin was the one man who would clear him of a murder charge, and this time no steel bars separated him from Duncan as had been the case with Jeremiah Parton back in Leesville. He meant to get the truth out of this one if he had to half kill him to do it.

They came to a coarse stand of mountain laurel and buckbrush. Here, too, was some fire plant and some wiry sage interspersed with high country, red-barked manzanita. Duncan made their horses fast here and instructed Marianne to stay close enough to clamp a hand over their nostrils should they hear or smell that other animal and attempt to call out. She seemed, for the first time, to be uneasy. Duncan noticed this and it annoyed him. He frowned over at her.

"Dog-gone it, girl," he said roughly. "You've

held up fine so far. Don't go getting all rubbery-legged now."

Marianne's eyes flashed fire points. "If you think I'm afraid, you're badly mistaken."

"You're giving a pretty good imitation of it," he growled. "Now, you listen to me . . . if he gets out of that cussed shack, I'll try and head him off. But if I can't, if he gets away, I'm going to have to concentrate on keeping him away from his horse. That means he'll probably try to get our horses. If you see anything at all that looks suspicious . . . shoot. You understand?"

"Of course I understand. Do you propose to stand here talking all night?"

"It's morning," Duncan said, hoisting the carbine.

"All right . . . all morning then."

He made a slow smile at her. This was better, he thought, knowing she was mad. He tipped his hat, stepped away, turned, and swung along through the forest fringe going back around to the front of that slowly decaying, old, log house.

The moon left, sinking behind a thick mountain battlement. On Duncan's right stars still lay thick in that still water twenty-acre lake. Parton's grazing horse was moving leisurely downcountry in the direction where their horses had been when he'd scented them before. This pleased Duncan. The farther from the cabin the animal went the better.

A porcupine, evidently attracted by the salty scent of horse sweat on leather, came grumpily waddling along. It never did actually see Duncan with its weak, watery eyes, but it smelled him, halted, bristled, made its bitterly complaining grunting sounds, then went protestingly on its way.

CHAPTER TWELVE

A panther screamed from the overhead heights, bringing the hair along Duncan's neck erect. He thought the big cat had probably scented that grazing horse and had been stalking him on his downward prowl, when man scent had also come up to him, making the cougar both fearful and angry.

He knew Marianne had also heard that eerie cry and bleakly smiled to himself at his imagined view of her face about now—white as a sheet, where she stood with their nervous horses, alone except for the loaded six-gun.

Silence resettled after the panther's scream, seeming deeper than before, as though every forest dweller was now rigid, waiting and intently listening. The big cat was the enemy of every high-country creature except the bear. He was the most dreaded killer of them all.

That scream had brought the unseen man within his log shelter to life. Duncan heard him in there. He got low behind a deadfall with Marianne's carbine, waiting. Range men, hearing a panther cry close by in the night, went forth at once to see after their livestock, fully armed.

Duncan waited. Time ran on. The man in the old cabin did not emerge, and gradually Duncan relaxed. Perhaps young Parton's shoulder was troubling him. It had been an arduous climb even for Duncan who had no serious injury. For a man with a shoulder wound it would have been both difficult and painful.

Duncan wished the cougar would scream again, but it never did. He speculated on the best way to cross to the cabin and concluded that the only feasible way would be to belly-crawl forward following out the tallest grassy growth. But, should young Parton be watching, he could not avoid seeing Duncan's progress because the only moving thing in sight would be quivering grass stands.

Short of a direct charge across the starlit meadow, there was no other way. Duncan balanced this decision and held off making it, at least until he saw how approaching dawn was bringing a steely brightness to this lonely world. Then he decided to make the run, not to prolong the anxiety by stalking the cabin.

He was rising up from behind the deadfall, when from the corner of his eye he sighted blurred movement off on his right. He instantly dropped down again, whipped the Winchester around, and held his breath.

It was Marianne. She came along without making a sound. He let her get within ten feet before speaking. It took that long for the anger in him to diminish a little.

"Here," he whispered, when she was close enough to hear. "Here, behind this deadfall. What in the hell possessed you? I explicitly told you to stay with our horses. What're you trying to do . . . let the entire world know where we are?"

She got down close to him, swung her face so that soft star shine touched down upon it, and whispered vehemently: "I doubt if the entire world is interested. If you'll just shut up for a minute, I'll tell you why I left the horses . . . you didn't think I'd do that because I got lonely, did you?"

"I . . ."

"Because if you did, Todd Duncan, let me tell you something . . . I'd rather be friendly with that mountain lion than with you, or with anyone like you."

"Did you slip over here to tell me that? It could've . . ."

"I slipped over here . . . if you'll be quiet long enough to let me get a word in . . . to tell you there are riders coming up our back trail."

Duncan stared.

"I thought I heard them about twenty minutes ago. Then, just before I came over here, I distinctly heard shod horses splash across that little white-water creek a mile or so back. Now, are you satisfied?"

Duncan pursed his lips, raised up to put a thoughtful look out over the ghostly meadow, and swung his face with a gathering frown, back to the onward cabin.

"Berryhill and Thorne," he muttered, bringing his head back down where he could look levelly at Marianne. "Sure as the devil. How many horses?"

"At least three and perhaps six or seven. I couldn't tell."

"Berryhill, Thorne, and a damned posse from Leesville."

"Probably. What do we do now? They'll be into the meadow in another twenty minutes." She was watching Duncan's face intently.

"We get inside that blasted cabin, get Parton, and hand him over to the law. That's what we do."

"How?" she asked, swinging to look across the open intervening meadow.

"Like this," Duncan said, fiercely pushing back upright and hefting the carbine, balancing there, making his hard decision, and putting his full attention upon the rotting old cabin. "You cover me. If he shoots, shoot back . . . but be careful. I don't cherish the notion of stopping one from behind as well as in front."

"Todd, don't be foolish. Wait for Sheriff Berryhill."

"Who's being foolish? I can't wait. Suppose young Parton lies about me like his father did?"

"How could he? After all, you're not . . ."

"Never mind the wherefores, Marianne," broke

in Duncan. "Just give me cover fire if he opens up."

She parted her lips to cry out to him, then checked herself as he sprang over the deadfall and sprinted out through the final tree fringe to the meadow beyond, picked up speed as he ran on, twisting first in one direction, then in another direction.

The distance was not excessive but it seemed to Marianne to be limitless. She drew the six-gun, cocked it, and kneeled across the old deadfall, watching him cover that eerily lit broad expanse. She could even hear his footfalls, the swish of tall grass against his trouser legs, and the little tinkling sound of the carbine's saddle ring.

Then he was against the cabin's front wall, shoulders flat against the logs, Winchester steady in both hands, waiting.

It was an interminable wait to Marianne, but actually Duncan, pressed as he was for time, did not linger very long waiting for the shot that never came. He stepped close, lifted one booted foot, and violently kicked the sagging old door. It went inward with a grinding sound, broke off one hinge, and quivered.

From inside came a man's sharp gasp.

"Drop it!" Duncan barked around the door-jamb. "Toss it out here, Parton . . . and be damned quick about it!"

Instead of a gun sailing through the door, a

man's agitated voice said: "This ain't Parton . . . whoever he is. This here is Ace Hopkins of the Flyin' L outfit, and whoever you are out there, I don't have no gun, so come on in and cut these damned ropes off me."

Duncan stood there dumbfounded. That voice had a ring of irate truthfulness to it. He pushed his Winchester around, waited, then followed the gun barrel in.

The smell of this old cabin was as rank with moldiness as that underground, abandoned room beneath Leesville's jailhouse was. It was dark, too, not as dark as was that other place, but dark enough for Duncan not to catch sight of the bound man upon the earthen floor until he writhed and cursed.

Duncan went close, dropped down, and looked into this stranger's face. He flicked back the man's jacket to stare at his uninjured right shoulder. Finally, with the wrathful cowboy swearing, he cut him loose where someone had securely bound the man with his own lariat.

"Who're you?" the cowboy asked, sitting up, making a wry face and beginning to rub his wrists. "What the hell's goin' on around here tonight, anyway? I been puttin' up at this line camp for five years, and tonight I've run into more folks in this meadow than I ever have in all those other five years put together."

The cowboy suddenly stopped exercising his

wrists. He looked past Duncan and his mouth fell open. Duncan twisted, saw Marianne step inside, and swung back to continue casting off the sliced ropes.

"A girl," the rider said, almost reverently. "Now, by golly, I've seen everythin'."

Duncan pulled the man to his feet and steadied him. "You just think you've seen everything," he muttered. "What happened to you?"

"I don't know exactly. I was fixin' to make a little supper, when out of nowhere comes this tall, lanky fellow with his six-gun on me. He made me finish cookin'. He ate like a horse, then he made me lie down, and he tied me with my own blamed rope."

"Did he have a hurt shoulder?"

The cowboy looked over at Duncan. "He sure did. He'd been shot. I lay there on the floor, watchin' him tear up my only clean shirt, makin' a bandage. It wasn't a real bad wound, but it seemed to trouble him some. Looked to me, in the poor light, to be maybe three, four weeks old."

"Is that his horse outside?"

"I reckon it is, mister. At least he told me he was goin' to trade critters with me, because mine was fresh and his wasn't."

"He didn't happen to mention his name, did he?"

"No. He took my shell belt, my six-gun, my horse, and lit out."

"How long was he here?"

The cowboy shrugged. "Couple hours maybe. Maybe a little more. I didn't pay much attention to the time. I was too blamed surprised at what was going on. Tell me, mister . . . was he some fellow on the dodge?"

"Yeah, he shot the expressman down at Leesville a few days back."

"No," said the cowboy, his eyes getting round. "Then I expect I was lucky."

"Very lucky. Which way did he ride out, do you know?"

"I didn't see him leave, but I can tell you this, mister, there's only two ways in and two ways out. If you come up the trail by that fry-pan lake and didn't meet him, then he had to go out over the rimrocks."

Duncan stood there. lost in thought for a moment. He swung toward Marianne saying: "You know the rimrock trail?" When she nodded, he added: "Then let's get moving."

As the pair of them crossed over to the door, the Flying L rider said: "Hey, what's the hurry? I got plenty of grub. We can eat, then I'll go with you."

"No time," Duncan said, pausing upon the rotting little porch to listen to the southward run of country. "There'll be a posse along here within the next few minutes. Cook up some breakfast for them."

He and Marianne left, not bothering to skirt

back around through the trees now, but making directly across the faintly lit meadow to their horses. As they were untying their horses, Duncan caught the quick sharp sound of a shod hoof striking stone. Marianne heard it, also. They exchanged a look, swung up, and reined off deeper into the trees, heading west now, with Marianne taking the lead.

For a while the land gently lifted toward a hanging bench where manzanita stood as thick as iron railings and just about as penetrable. They found a buck run that was scarcely wide enough for their passage, pushed their way through it to more open country beyond, and halted upon that shadowy hillside to glance back.

Horsemen were passing directly over the big meadow heading for the line-camp cabin. They looked small down there and slow-moving. Dawn was abroad elsewhere, but in this mountainous world only the steely hint of its approach lay outward and downward, drenching the world in a gun metal color that was becoming gradually diluted to a watery, lusterless gray that tolerated no shadows. In some places a nighttime darkness still lingered, lying darkly like heavy smoke, obscuring those hard stone cañons and bleak drop-offs.

Duncan counted six horsemen in the posse. He could not see any of the men well enough to recognize them, but it occurred to him that

Berryhill and Thorne probably had those same four men with them as a nucleus they'd had when they'd taken Duncan the first time. He turned his horse, thinking bitterly that they'd never get him again as easily as they had at the cottonwood spring.

"Lead out," he said to Marianne. "Where would he go now . . . with extra guns, plenty of ammunition, and a fresh horse?"

"There is only one way he can go. At least for the next three miles. After that, with any kind of luck, we ought to be able to either track him or see him. We'll stay to the rimrocks."

"Fine," Duncan said, taking up his reins.

But Marianne did not rein out. She said: "Give me one good reason why you won't let Berryhill help us in this?"

"Sure," he said tartly. "One good reason is that, if Berryhill and Thorne get me again, they'll send me back."

"But they'll know the minute that Flying L cowboy tells them what happened to him, that Parton's son *is* the one they want."

"That won't prevent them from sending me back until they get this thing ironed out."

"What difference does that make, Todd? Sheriff Berryhill will do the chasing and we won't have to."

Duncan put a wry look across at Marianne. "Listen, young lady, it's *me* that dang' near got lynched down there. It's me that's been jailed and cussed at and worried to a frazzle. Therefore it's going to be *me* who's in at the end of this chase. If Berryhill and Thorne want to be in on it, too, that's their affair. But by golly, I've had about all the roughing up a man has to take before he starts fighting back. Now either lead out or get out of the trail."

Marianne turned, eased her mount out, and didn't say another word. She rocketed along where the land sharply lifted, turned abruptly east, and, with Duncan following grimly, the pair of them passed beyond sight of the meadow below.

Chapter Thirteen

They were paralleling that abrupt stone precipice that faced the hidden meadow to the south, curving out around it so neither they, nor the meadow below and behind them, were visible. Their trail was another of those buck runs, but here they encountered enough bear sign to warn them they were in a primitive area where few people ventured and where the mighty black and brown bears of the uplands reigned.

Marianne rode along with the confidence and ease of a person acquainted with this country, and Duncan marveled that she would ever have been up in here. It was neither an easy place to reach nor one that would appeal to most women.

When they began bending on around behind that stony mountainside, coming upon the broader, grassier spine of it, they again encountered immense stands of first-growth pines, and the silence was cathedral-like.

Duncan alternately watched the land ahead and the trail underfoot. It was clear that a horse had been ridden along here not long before. He felt that as long as young Parton did not leave the trail, they would have no difficulty tracking him down. It did not occur to him for some time in this kind of riding that Parton might have stopped upon some stony headland to watch his back trail. But when he did think this might be so, he put Marianne behind him and took the lead, watching each promontory ahead of them with particular care.

Riding like this, they encountered some belled cattle. The way these animals acted convinced Duncan the man he was after had also ridden through here. They did not turn tail and run as cattle ordinarily did after seeing their first humans after months of being alone in the highlands. Instead, they threw up their heads and stood watching, motionlessly.

Marianne came up to Duncan as they began descending toward a far mountainside with a waterfall silvering its bony side. There was another of those secret parks between them and the waterfall. From their descending height they could see down into that meadow.

"That's an old Indian camp ground down there," she told Duncan. "And along the base of that cliff, where the waterfall is, there are some caves. If Parton took his time, he might have found one of them."

Duncan considered what Marianne had said. As long as young Parton had no idea that he was being this closely pursued, and with the discomfort of his wound, he might very well have decided to rest in that park. Duncan halted while they were still halfway down off the hillside, in among a ragged and gloomy stand of old trees, to survey the meadow, seeking to find a horse down there. He saw several deer and two stag elks but no horse.

He raised his gaze to include the rugged onward escarpments, and Marianne, reading his mind, said: "Those high peaks are the top out. From there he'd be descending the far side toward the plains beyond. If he didn't stop, then within another few hours he'll be over the top and probably out of our reach."

Duncan turned. "Why out of our reach?"

Marianne shrugged. "If he can make the plains, he'll walk away from us on that fresh horse. Our animals are tiring."

Duncan looked at their mounts, swore under his breath, and pushed on.

They continued down the hillside to the last row of trees before entering the meadow, made another little rest halt while Duncan again studied the surrounding grassy meadow. Marianne thought he would dismount as he'd done before and scout the place afoot, but Duncan reined off at a leisurely walk, leading the way on around the meadow, staying back several hundred feet in the surround-ing forest where he could see out without being seen himself.

An hour later they were within hearing distance of that waterfall's dull roar. Here, Duncan found another of those highland lakes. He stopped to gaze a moment at the lucid water, understanding why Indians would cherish this place, then turned sharply as Marianne spoke his name in a loud whisper.

She was pointing westward along the stone face, past the waterfall. Duncan looked, saw nothing, and swung back with a gathering frown.

"What is it?"

"A horse," she said. "There . . . follow along the cliff. Watch for movement against those backdrop trees."

Duncan did and spotted the animal. It seemed to be standing, facing into the forest as though it might be tied there. What made it difficult to discern was that its dark color blended perfectly with the shadowy growth around it.

"Has a saddle on," breathed Duncan. He swung down, looped his reins, drew out Marianne's carbine, and hefted it. At that moment the two stag elks they had spotted earlier flung up their great heads, clearly alarmed by something they had scented or seen, and in a flash went bounding out of the meadow into the shielding forest.

"He's over there," Duncan said as Marianne stepped down from her horse. She tied her animal and moved closer to him as he said: "But he's showing caution."

"He might be thinking that cowboy back at the line camp could have gotten loose by now," Marianne opined.

"Maybe," agreed Duncan. "Come on. We can't ride back around the meadow or his horse'll smell our animals. We'll have to walk it."

They reversed their course because where that waterfall fell, there was no protecting growth at all. If they had gone directly across the meadow, they would certainly have been sighted.

Duncan walked with thrusting strides. At first Marianne had no particular difficulty keeping up, but after a while, panting, she asked Duncan to rest a moment. He did so, but with increasing annoyance. He was thinking that Berryhill's posse could descend into this place while they were a mile away from their horses, and that since the cowboy Duncan had cut loose would undoubtedly tell the lawman which route they were taking, Berryhill's riders could make even better time getting over here than had Duncan and Marianne.

He started on again, finally, without a word, leaving it up to Marianne whether or not she would go along with him. She went, but she shot him an indignant look as they started out again.

It took considerable time, even with the punishing gait Duncan set, to encircle the meadow on foot and get within easy sighting distance of that saddled animal. Duncan finally halted a quarter mile off, grounded his Winchester, and nodded.

"He's tied all right, Marianne. Tied to a pine

sapling. That wasn't real smart of Parton, though, tying his critter with its rump out into the meadow."

It did not occur to Duncan that this might not have been any accident. That in fact it might have been a definite lure, leaving that saddled horse out where it would be seen, and investigated, by anyone riding through.

"He must be lying back in the trees over there," said Marianne, pointing. "There's a little creek not far from where the horse is. Maybe he's resting there."

Duncan nodded, said—"We'll edge up a little closer."—and resumed his advance, but more slowly now, being especially careful to make no sound and to present as little of himself as he could, staying in the deeper shadows of the forest and keeping Marianne always behind him.

Once, that saddled horse raised its head looking westward, but whether it had heard anything or not, it did not seem particularly disturbed and shortly after this dropped its head and resumed its drowsing stance.

Duncan got a good look at the beast from three hundred feet off. It did not look very fresh to him. In fact, it looked as ridden down as his own horse. He twisted to murmur to Marianne: "The Flying L cowboy's got an odd idea of what a fresh horse is."

She said nothing back. She was also considering

that tethered beast, only she was frowning, looking puzzled and curious. She seemed, after a long moment, to be on the verge of speaking, but at the same moment Duncan put back a rigid arm warning her to stillness. She forgot the horse at once, sensing from Duncan's stiffening stance that something was wrong. She strained over his shoulder, searching for whatever it was that had alerted him.

A half-grown black bear came ambling out of the deeper forest, making its grunting, complaining sounds. It shambled along swinging its head unconcernedly from side to side. Once, it halted to tear at the rotting bark of a small deadfall pine, sniffed for grubs, then stepped on over the little tree and shuffled another hundred feet ahead, its weak eyes seeing only what was close but its sensitive nose constantly wrinkling. Then, very suddenly, it stopped, threw up its head, keened the air for a moment, then reared back on its hind legs, coming up off the ground to increase its sniffing height. It was as tall as a man and weighed about six hundred pounds. In itself it was not dangerous, or at least it wasn't dangerous unless it thought it was threatened. But clearly now, it had caught an alarming scent, for the hair along its back stood straight up.

Watching with his entire attention, Duncan thought the bear had smelled man. He'd seen his share of wild bears, knew from experience how they reacted to the scent of people, and this one was acting true to form.

The bear dropped back down on all fours, pointed southward beyond the tethered horse, and Duncan thought he knew about where the owner of that horse was. He bent cautiously, picked up a round stone, threw it, and when it struck the bear's ribs he gave an astonished grunt, looked fleetingly in Duncan's direction, then swung around and went running off back the way he had come.

Parton's tethered horse, though, was no longer drowsing. He'd unmistakably caught the smell of a bear. He was trembling and fighting his tether. It seemed to Duncan that he would break loose at any moment. It puzzled him that young Parton was not coming out to investigate that stamping and frightened snorting, but he did not appear. For a little while longer this roiled atmosphere went unchanged.

Marianne put her lips close to Duncan's ear and said: "He's south of us the way that bear was looking. You go ahead and I'll stay back here and cover you."

Duncan turned. Their faces were very close. The bear had not frightened her, he could see that, yet she was troubled by something else. He mistakenly thought it was the tension in this gloomy, perilous place, and he smiled at her, his first smile at Marianne Dudley since he'd met her.

"You're quite a girl," he whispered back, and saw surprise widen her eyes. "When we get out of this, I'll apologize for being mean to you." His smile broadened, deepened, then he swung away. Over his shoulder he said: "All right . . . just remember which one is me, if you have to shoot."

He left her, paced a hundred feet onward, swung to look back at her, and discovered that she had dropped down, and because of her dark attire and the gloominess of this place, he could no longer see her at all even though he knew exactly where to look.

He eased ahead furtively, came abreast of the tethered horse, watched the beast's diminishing nervousness, and stepped farther to his right so as to be deeper in forest shadows.

A definite uneasiness began to nag at his awareness. He stopped, rummaged the roundabout places for a man shape, found none, and swung to look out at the horse. There was something definitely wrong. Young Parton had not rushed out when his horse was close to setting him afoot miles from anywhere. He had not even made any attempt to chase the bear away, and now, although he'd obviously come here in a hurry and thought it unwise to offsaddle, he was wasting precious time as though he had no troubles at all.

It occurred to Duncan that Parton's shoulder

might be weakening him. Perhaps the killer was lying back somewhere near, sleeping.

Out of nowhere an exultant voice struck Duncan squarely in the back: "Drop that gun and freeze, mister!"

Duncan jerked up stiffly. His knuckles tightened around the Winchester. He half twisted from the waist to look behind.

"Mister, you make one more move and I'll kill you. Now drop that gun!"

Realization came finally. Duncan had been adroitly trapped. That horse tethered out in the open, instead of back beyond view in the forest, had been Parton's bait to draw anyone on.

He did not know young Parton and yet that sharp, menacing voice behind him coming from among the gloomy old trees was familiar. He put out his arm, leaned the Winchester against it, and dropped his arm, waiting. He wanted a good look at his captor. For the moment he had entirely forgotten Marianne.

A man's spurred boots came stepping carefully forward, passing warily far out around Duncan from back to front. Once, they halted as though the unseen gunman was carefully inspecting Duncan from a distance for other guns. Then they continued on until, by turning his head the slightest bit, Duncan caught the blur of movement, and, a moment later, the definite lank, lean, easy-moving silhouette of a rider as tall as Duncan came into view. Again, something stirred in Duncan's mind. This man, whoever he was, was definitely familiar.

Then Duncan saw him. It was the youngest of those three tall posse men Sheriff Berryhill had brought with him to the cottonwood spring when Duncan had first been arrested. The man who'd argued so fiercely in favor of hanging Duncan. He remembered this one's name now—Tom Black. He remembered something else, too. This one was a killer!

Black stepped into full view and he was smiling broadly. "Walked right into it, didn't you?" he chortled. "Couldn't resist investigatin' a tied horse, could you?"

CHAPTER FOURTEEN

Black's smile was menacing. The look in his eyes was deadly. "Can't figure how I got here so fast, can you?" he said to Duncan. "Well, I lit out from the line rider's cabin without even dismountin'. That's how. Berryhill and the others'll be along directly. They was tuckered and in need of some breakfast. Not me, though. When I'm getting close to my prey, I don't let up a minute."

This answered the question in Duncan's mind concerning that tired-looking tethered horse out there. It also told him something else as well. This man, Tom Black, for all his youthful appearance, was no one to joke with when he had a cocked six-gun in his fist, as he now had.

"One question," Duncan said when the other man ceased speaking. "How did Berryhill get up here so fast? The last I saw of him, he was wandering around in the dark, last night, and he was a long way from town."

"He didn't have to go plumb back to Leesville," Black answered, "because after we got inside the jailhouse, found you fellows was gone, some of us saddled up and headed out. I was with the boys who come onto the sheriff and Jack Thorne comin' back."

"And how did you know to come up in here looking for me?"

"That warn't no problem. Sheriff Berryhill had that old preacher in tow. He found him ridin' back, too."

"What did he do with old Parton?"

"Your paw? Why, we had to fetch him along." Black's wide lips lifted wolfishly. "He wouldn't trust none of us to take the old devil back to town for fear we'd hang him on the way, and you know . . . we would've."

Looking at this lank, sinewy man, it dawned on Duncan that he still believed Duncan was old Jeremiah Parton's son. "Did you get it out of old Parton that his boy's got a bullet in his shoulder?" he asked to focus his captor's attention upon both his own unwounded shoulders. It was a useless question.

Tom Black wagged his head. "Didn't talk to the old cuss," he replied. "Berryhill kept him up front between him and Jack Thorne. Like I already told you, Matt figured if any of us got our hands on him, we'd string him up."

Black would not know, then, that Duncan was not the old outlaw's son. But Duncan had only a slight hope otherwise, so this did not occupy his mind very long. He knew Marianne was behind him somewhere with her six-gun. Although he began fervently to hope that she would not brace Tom Black because he was

143

clearly a man who would shoot at the drop of a hat.

As it turned out, Marianne was in a position that was safe from a dozen hair-triggered killers. She had gotten around Black and was behind him when Duncan saw her. Only a slice of her was visible around an old fir tree with a huge bole. Nevertheless, Duncan's heart nearly stopped when she cocked that gun.

Black straightened up very gradually at that sharp, unpleasant little snippet of sound behind him. Duncan watched his eyes steadily brighten and widen as though he meant to whirl. Duncan diverted him with words.

"You'll be a fool to try it," he cautioned Black. "At that distance you'll get the big one right between the shoulder blades." He paused, waited for slack to come into the tall cowboy's frame, and when it finally came, he said: "Drop the gun. It was a good trap. You best be satisfied that you baited me into it. And by the way, Black, I'm not old man Parton's son. I've told you that before. If you'd asked Jeremiah Parton, you'd know that by now. If he told you the truth, that is."

Black listened. He eased off the hammer of his cocked pistol, let the weapon sag from his trigger finger, but he did not drop it.

Watching Black's eyes, Duncan saw what was passing through the other man's mind a second ahead of the violent eruption.

Black let out a defiant bawl and launched himself straight across the intervening distance at Duncan. He was gambling that whoever was behind would not dare shoot for fear of hitting Duncan. It was a good gamble. Marianne stood there, undecided and helpless, watching what was playing out.

Duncan had seen Black make his decision and was moving even as the cowboy hurled forward. He was clear of Black, who rushed past, when the cowboy came wide around, fists up, face pale, and his eyes mirroring a primitive lust to battle.

Marianne rushed forward to hand Duncan the six-gun. He brushed her back with an outflung arm. "Keep it," he told her. "He wants it this way and I aim to oblige him. He's one of 'em that wanted to lynch me."

Marianne got back but still held her six-gun. She saw Black start forward again, this time moving cattily, upon the pads of his feet with his sinewy body balanced forward to spring.

Duncan saw this, too, and he smiled over at his enemy.

"You try that lunging again," he told Black, "and I'll tear your jaw off."

The cowboy made a death's-head grin right back. "When I'm through with you, there won't be enough for the buzzards to quarrel over."

They circled, jabbing a little, stepping in and stepping out, neither willing to give the other any advantage, at all. Duncan dropped low, ran a looping blow under Black's guard that struck him lightly in the middle, jumped back, and avoided a lashing, wild strike that struck only air.

Twice more Duncan did this, each time stinging his adversary. He also taunted Black with words, bringing the other man's anger to a high pitch, making Black reckless in his eagerness to get hands upon Duncan.

Duncan swung away from two strikes, landed a short blow along Black's face that brought claret to the cowboy's nostrils, danced away, and continued his taunting.

Black rushed in, head low, with both arms flailing. Duncan turned sideways to avoid being struck, but Black, anticipating this, swung, also. That was when he caught Duncan flush with a bony fist, making stars burst inside Duncan's skull.

Seeing he had scored, Black pressed in, flailing away. He had no science, was not in fact even a very good barroom brawler, but he had courage and strength, and, after hurting Duncan, he kept slamming away, using both hands.

Duncan jumped left, jumped right. He was struck by only a few of those blows but each one hurt. He sprang back out of range and traded space for time until his head cleared, then, tasting bile and anger in about equal parts, he braced both legs wide, let Black come to him, and met sinew with sinew and bone with bone.

It was a punishing exchange that no two men could have prolonged, but Duncan was willing to have it this way. He did not propose to give a yard and he didn't, even though Black's fists hammered mercilessly at him, causing pain and, after thirty seconds had passed, a kind of numbness to his middle and his upper body.

But Black, equally as dogged, was not as seasoned at this kind of fighting as was Duncan. He took two savage strikes in the face. More claret sprayed. He took a terrific hammering in the belly, and finally dropped his arms to protect himself. The moment he did that, Duncan caught him flush on the jaw with a blasting right hand. Black staggered, gave ground, stumbled away, and heavily shook his head, both arms temporarily down.

Duncan went after him. The breathing of these two sounded to Marianne like a whipsaw standing head-on into a high wind. That, and the crunching of their booted feet, was the only sound.

Duncan tried to catch Black while he was groggy but failed. Black's instincts told him to run, and he did, back-pedaling, switching positions, swinging sideways, and all the time his mind was clearing. He stopped once to get his right shoulder down behind a cocked fist, but Duncan feinted him into prematurely firing that blow, then got past it to lean fiercely into the barrage of strikes he sunk, wrist-deep, into Black's bruised belly.

Marianne clearly heard the meaty sound of these strikes. She put her free hand to her lips in anguish.

Black started to go slack. He struck out but there was no power left and his timing was off—he'd try for a hit when Duncan was already weaving away. Black was hurt. Duncan knew this and jumped ahead to finish him. He caught the cowboy coming in uncertainly with a right hand. He nearly toppled him with a jabbing left hand. He stepped in, dropped, and threw his entire weight into a sledge-hammer blow that made Black's air rush out in a whooshing gasp. Black was doubled over by this one and his eyes were fixed aimlessly upon the ground as though they no longer focused.

Marianne called out, but Duncan ignored this to take one short step in closer. He tapped Black's shoulder, and when the gunman twisted his head, Duncan hit him with everything he had left, along the jaw. Black went down as though axed. His face was bloody, his fists were raw, and his frame was limp and raggedly heaving.

Duncan stood there a moment longer, looking down. He stooped, unbuckled Black's shell belt, strapped it on himself, and unsteadily made his way toward Marianne.

She led him deeper into the forest where a little mossy creek ran, and there his legs gave out. He went down on both knees and hung there, sucking the insufficient high-country air into his lungs.

Marianne used a neckerchief to bathe Duncan's face. She was pale from throat to hairline but she did not say a single word. Some ten minutes passed, and Duncan pushed upright, flexed his bruised knuckles, swung to gaze out through the tree trunks where Tom Black lay sprawled.

He said: "I feel better. In fact, I feel a *lot* better. I've had a hankering to do that to *someone* ever since Berryhill arrested me."

Marianne rinsed her neckerchief, stood up, and replied: "You don't *look* better, and I think if what he said is true, we'd better get back to our horses."

"Yeah," Duncan growled, shuffling out where the unconscious cowboy lay. "But first I've got one more little chore to do."

He passed Tom Black, went out to his tethered horse, methodically offsaddled, removed the bridle, and gave the gaunt beast a light pat on the rump.

Marianne protested. "He's hurt, Todd. You can't expect him to walk all the way back to Leesville in his condition, can you?"

"Come on," Duncan said angrily, watching Black's horse trot out where the tall meadow grass grew. "We've got to get out of here before the rest of that damned posse gets down here."

"But . . ."

Duncan turned. "I don't expect him to do anything," he growled, looking past Marianne at Tom Black. "He can walk back or fly back . . . or stay right there . . . for all I care. Now, are you coming with me or not?"

Duncan swung away hiking wearily back through the encircling trees in the direction of their horses. Marianne did not immediately follow him. She stooped to listen to the ragged breathing of Tom Black as she shot an indignant look at Duncan's disappearing broad shoulders in among the trees. She pursed her lips disapprovingly, then went hurrying after Duncan.

They got back to their horses with one more six-gun than they had when they'd left them about a half hour before. Duncan examined Black's gun, found it fully loaded, shoved it back into his waistband, and began rummaging a shirt pocket for his tobacco sack.

Marianne watched him work up a cigarette with his swelling, injured hands, light it, and bend a long look back up the westerly hillside for sign of Berryhill's posse. He still had the primeval, smoky look in his eyes of a man ready to fight. She wisely stood there watching him but saying nothing.

After a moment of smoking, Duncan removed

the cigarette, trickled smoke up his bruised face, solemnly looked down at her—and smiled.

"Pretty brutal, wasn't it?" he asked softly, looking at her face shaded by the trees around her. "I reckon you figure I'm cruel as all get out." He nodded his head at her, still smiling. "Well, I am, dammit, and I've got reason to be. And anyway, you said down in that arroyo last night you wanted a tough man . . . so if you want to shed a tear for Tom Black, go ahead and do it. But when I finish this cigarette, we'll be moving on, so don't waste a lot of time with your crying."

Marianne's face turned granite-like. She rasped at him: "Todd Duncan, I hate you!"

He put the cigarette back between his lips, inhaled deeply, exhaled, and nodded gravely. "I don't blame you. Sometimes I sort of hate myself. What I should've done over there was put a bullet through his danged skull." At Marianne's swift, shocked look of incredulity, he said in the same easy, conversational voice: "Sure, he was going to kill me before you cocked that gun behind him. I could read it in his face as plain as day, woman. Now, I operate by a code that says when someone aims to kill you, you got as good a right to kill them."

"You'd be as bad as an Indian if you did that, and you know it."

Duncan took a last long drag off the cigarette. She heard the deep sweep of smoke in his chest.

151

He dropped the stub and ground it out. He was beginning to feel better. The aches were there and the pains, but his strength was fast returning and he could afford to look out at her from beneath his curling hat brim and make a crooked little grin.

"Maybe you're right," he drawled. "Maybe I should've just stomped his rib cage in." He turned away from her and nodded toward her horse. "Get astride, girl. We've wasted enough time here." He untied his own animal, toed in, and sprang up. Without looking back to see whether she was mounted or not, he started riding off.

CHAPTER FIFTEEN

They passed along the face of that southward cliff out beyond where the waterfall's spray might reach, riding west through stirrup-high meadow grass with morning dew still on it.

The grayness was entirely gone now. A brightness lay upon the land, bringing on the warmth of the new day and aiding visibility. For a while they seemed to be the only people abroad in this day, then Duncan saw the lazy drift of dust rising upon the northward hillside where riders were angling down into the meadow. He pointed it out to Marianne, at the same time altering course a little so as to make it into the yonder forest quicker.

She protested, saying they were heading away from the caves at the base of the cliff. His answer to this was elemental. If there was no horse hereabouts, he said to her, then young Parton was not here, either, because he'd ridden into this place, and if he was resting in a cave somewhere, his horse would be close by, which it obviously wasn't. He added that they'd ridden completely around the meadow, had walked back through the trees, and were now riding openly over the meadow, and still they hadn't come across a horse.

Marianne said no more until, back into the tree fringe, she struck the onward trail again. She made a close scrutiny for a thousand yards, found the tracks of young Parton's animal, straightened up in the saddle, and, without a word, followed them.

Duncan saw all this and smiled, thinking that a proud woman, like a proud man, had difficulty admitting error. But a proud woman was also a strong woman. He was satisfied, not only that he'd been right in his surmise concerning the killer they were seeking, but also in his companion in this hunt.

They began climbing, first steeply then angling, until they emerged into a cleared place high above the park and its waterfall. Duncan signaled for a halt, twisted to look back, and saw the bunched-up band of riderless horses down below where they'd left Tom Black.

"Let's go," he said. "They've found him." He returned his attention to the tiers of trees marching in ranks up toward the craggy, wind-scoured top out above them. "Would he stop again before pushing on over?" he asked.

Marianne was doubtful, but, pausing to think, she finally said: "There is one more little park up here."

"With water?"

"Yes. We'll look there. If he's not in that place, he'll have crossed over."

Duncan nodded, motioned for Marianne to ride on, and eased out behind her.

They rode a mile through the forest shadows

where sunlight occasionally came down in filtered shafts of golden hue. This was also a cathedral-like place—silent, still, timeless. If men had been here before them, they had not made this ride very often. Even the pine needles underfoot gave off a musty dust as they passed over them. It struck Duncan once more that Marianne had an unusual knowledge of this far country. He asked her about that.

She said: "My father loved to hunt. Every autumn he'd take me with him. We'd pack two horses and stay in the mountains, sometimes a month. I doubt if there are many places we didn't visit at one time or another."

"And you liked it?" he asked, wondering about her. He'd heard of precious few women in his lifetime who enjoyed roughing it.

Marianne nodded without looking back at him. "I loved it. It was as though we were the only people in the world. We didn't have to be adults. We picked wildflowers. We fished the ice water lakes. We laughed a lot and had no cares at all."

Duncan rode along after she said that, considering her. She was not the usual town girl in the least, he thought. Then she said something that clinched this opinion for him.

"The man who killed him was worse than an animal. Worse than that bear we saw or the panther we heard. They were predators, and yet they don't kill without reason."

"Young Parton thought he had a reason, Marianne. There was a fortune in the express company safe."

"Why didn't he just take it? My father wasn't armed and he offered no resistance." She looked around awaiting his answer to this.

He had none. At least no logical answer. "I'm not defending young Parton . . . I'm only giving you his reason." He returned her look, shrugged, and added: "It's never necessary to condone something people do, but it's necessary to understand why a thing was done in order to judge the man who did it."

She thought on this for a little distance, nodded acceptance, and asked: "And what is your judgment of my father's murderer?"

Duncan made a wide gesture with one hand indicating their surroundings. "I'm here with you, aren't I? What more proof do you need of how I feel about it?" He dropped his arm, returned her steady gaze, and added something to this: "But I think you want a swifter kind of justice than I want. Back there with Tom Black . . . I wouldn't have killed him. Shot him maybe, if he'd forced me to it . . . but killed him . . . no."

"You certainly let me believe you would have."

He grinned crookedly at her. "Yeah . . . don't ask me why I did that. All I can tell you is that when you seemed so horrified, I still was full of aches and pains, and meanness."

She put her skeptical gaze upon him, saying dryly: "Just the same I'm glad I wasn't Tom Black."

He let this pass. "Tell me something. Just who is Black, anyway?"

"A local cowboy. He rides for the big outfits and between jobs loafs in Leesville. He doesn't have the best reputation in town, but I've never heard anything really bad about him."

"Was he a particular friend of yours or your father's?"

"No, not really. He used to visit my father in the express office occasionally. They were both hunters."

"Well," Duncan wryly summarized, "I'll tell you this much . . . he's a killer, Marianne. I know his type very well. They'll kill when they have what to them appears to be a good reason."

"Don't forget," she retorted, "everyone in Leesville is very worked-up over my father's murder. Tom Black included. Just because you're safe in the mountains today doesn't mean that any of those people who wanted to lynch you yesterday have cooled off any. I'd say that back in Leesville right now there is even more wrath than there was yesterday. You escaped them. . . . They'll be angrier than ever about that."

"I'm wondering about Sheriff Berryhill. You heard Black say some of the men from town met him . . . that he's riding with them right now."

"What's wrong with that?"

"Marianne, those are the same men who were trying to lynch me yesterday. They're also the same men who were trying to shoot Berryhill and Jack Thorne in the jailhouse."

She swung forward, rode along a little ways, then turned back toward him again. "Sheriff Berryhill is a man who takes on one problem at a time. Right now he wants you. But I wouldn't want to be one of those men after he catches you. He's not a pleasant man when he's been crossed."

Duncan chuckled ruefully. "Most men aren't," he murmured. "Especially if they've been punched, shot at, cursed, and scared half to death."

Marianne understood this innuendo. She turned back to face forward and said no more until, with the trail passing over a wide, level bench, they entered one of those gaps that permitted a backward look. There she halted, knowing Duncan would wish to examine their back trail.

He looked outward and downward for a long time waiting for telltale dust. When it didn't show against the azure sky, he swung off, dropped the reins, and groped for his tobacco sack. He didn't look at Marianne even after she dismounted, strolled back, and stopped beside him. He lit up, fanned excess blue smoke with his hat, popped the cigarette between his lips, and stood patiently waiting. Sooner or later Berryhill's posse would stir up dust.

"They will be a long way back," opined Marianne. "Black wouldn't be fit to ride for twenty minutes at least, after they found him."

"Maybe," he commented. "And maybe some of the others did what Black did . . . struck out ahead of Berryhill and Thorne. That's what I want to see about before we go on."

For a while neither of them spoke. Duncan, wearying of his vigil after a time, swung to survey the onward peaks and forested shoulders. "How much farther to this next park where Parton might be?" he asked.

"Half a mile."

"Any caves up there?"

"No. We'll be able to see the entire park without leaving the forest. If he's there, we'll know it as soon as the place comes into view."

He dropped his gaze to her face. "You look tired," he said.

Without any hesitation she said right back: "You look like you need a shave, a bath, and some ointment where he hit you."

Duncan slowly grinned. Marianne returned that grin with a slow smile of her own. He took a long drag off his smoke, exhaled, and said: "You're the dog-gonedest female I ever ran across. I didn't believe they still made 'em like you."

This time there was hesitation before she retorted, and her level gaze faltered a little before that strongly masculine look of candid approval.

"How would you know what kind of females are in the world, following trail herds, passing through strange lands without even going into the towns, always on the move?"

He considered his cigarette, turned away from her to scan the back trail, before he said quietly: "Yeah, you're plumb right. . . . How would I know?" He dropped the smoke, stepped on it, shot her a grave look from beneath his tilted hat brim, and added: "Marianne, you suppose if I stayed around Leesville . . . ?"

"Dust," she said, cutting across his words and pointing downcountry.

He turned, studied the distant, faint spiraling of roiled air for a while, then nodded and turned back.

"Better be pushing on," he said gruffly, without looking at her.

She put out a tanned hand to restrain him. "Before I interrupted . . . what were you saying?"

He shook off her hand. "Something silly," he muttered as he stepped past and caught his horse. He swung the beast to him, raised up over leather, and gazed down at her. "Must be the altitude," he said, and reined away, taking the lead without waiting to see if she got astride.

She caught up with him a quarter mile from the

last hidden meadow this side of the rimrocks. "It's not the altitude," she said to his broad back. "It's just that you don't know what you want out of life . . . whether to accept some responsibility or be another fiddle-footed cowboy."

He reined up sharply, twisted, and scowled back at her. "You," he pronounced very distinctly, very acidly, "are the cussedest female I ever saw for roiling a man. If you were ten years younger, I'd bend you over my knee and wallop you with my reins. I know what I want out of life, and don't you think otherwise."

She said nothing, only motioned him to proceed along the trail as though she preferred to let this particular conversation die right where it was.

But Todd Duncan was not a man to be herded by others. She might have known that, if she'd paused to consider how he'd acted so far on this trail they were both riding. He was a thorough man who relied entirely upon himself in bad places. He sat there, blocking the trail, looking at her with strong displeasure.

For a long time this perplexing, troubled atmosphere remained between them, but finally she said: "All right. Have it your way. It's not my concern anyway. Now, from here on be careful. We'll be coming to the last park very shortly."

He ignored this, saying: "You know, I think a good larruping might be just what you need anyway, ten years older or not."

Chapter Sixteen

Duncan came to the final fringe of trees and halted well back to gaze ahead. It was in his mind that if young Parton was in the yonder meadow, his own position was no more enviable than the killer's was. Berryhill's posse was passing upcountry on this same trail, and they would have an advantage that they had not possessed until they got to the first meadow—Duncan's horse tracks.

Marianne came up to Duncan and stopped. He did not look around, his whole attention was fixed upon the sunlit place ahead.

This park, as these small upland meadows were called, was about thirty acres wide and roughly the same size in width. As in the other parks, trees completely surrounded the place cutting off all bright light that did not come directly downward. The grass here was lush and tall. There were meandering, thin game trails criss-crossing the place and next to the black-cut of a stone buttress rising to the north was a tiny seepage spring. The water here appeared to come directly out of smooth granite. Along the narrow run of this little creek tules and willows grew profusely, intermingling with one another and tall stands of rip-gut grass.

That was where Duncan spotted the rump of a big bay horse. The beast seemed to be drowsily picking at the creekbank. No more of him was visible than his heavy hindquarters. Marianne also saw him. Duncan heard her sucked-back, quick breath. Before she could speak, if that had been her intention, he solemnly nodded, telling her in this way he'd seen the animal.

He got down, motioned for her to do likewise, handed her his reins, saying: "Take 'em off through the trees and tie 'em out of sight. Take 'em far enough so they won't scent any horses coming up the trail and nicker."

Marianne nodded. She was staring hard over where that grazing horse was.

For a second he studied her profile, then a little wicked gleam showed in his eyes. He bent close and murmured: "About that larruping . . . I haven't forgotten."

Her head instantly whipped around toward him. She gave him a smoky stare and whispered the same thing she'd said before: "You just try it."

"All right," he assented, his wicked grin broadening. "But later . . . right now there's something more important to do."

He took the Winchester, jerked his head for her to lead the horses off, swung away, and started the same scouting maneuver around the forest fringe he'd used down in the first meadow. She lost sight of him almost at once.

A scolding blue jay appeared in the overhead treetops announcing raucously Duncan's presence to every forest creature. He stopped beside a rough-barked, old fir, glowered at this sentinel of the highlands, caught up a stone, and heaved it at the bird. The blue jay fled, keeping up its loud racket until distance softened it. Afterward, Duncan glided away from the spot where this had happened, inched up the meadow, and stood for several minutes while peering out, watching and waiting. Every rider of the highcountry trails knew the character of blue jays. They, as well as the wild creatures, knew that one of those scoldings meant something alien was close by.

But if young Parton knew this, he did not show himself to seek the cause of the turmoil. Even his grazing horse continued to crop grass, indifferent to the blue jay's excited jabberings.

Duncan sighed in quiet relief, stepped back deeper among the trees, and resumed his round-about pacing. With the blue jay's departure there was not a sound to be heard anywhere. This kind of stillness was in itself an omen to experienced range men, for normally there were upland birds and other creatures aplenty in the parks and forests. Their very absence was significant. Something had frightened them off.

Duncan felt, all things considered, that his quest was nearing its end. He slowed his approach where the black bulwark stood, prohibiting any further travel southward. He squatted behind a sage thicket and blocked in squares of the area ahead, seeking, not so much the shape of a man, as the signs that would indicate that a man was somewhere close by.

He did not find these telltale bent fronds, trampled places, broken rip-gut stalks, until sometime later when the browsing horse stepped back, half swung away from Duncan, and lifted its head in a listening posture.

Where that animal had been standing, obscuring Duncan's view, was a trampled pathway leading to the creek and beyond it through a tangle of wild underbrush. There were ample indications that a man, as well as a horse, had gone through the man-high growth there.

Duncan was satisfied. He pulled himself upright, hefted the Winchester, balanced the idea in his mind of trying to approach that hiding place, and decided instead to go back to make certain the pursuit was not close. He also wanted to bring Marianne back with him. His reason for this was simple. He not only felt responsible for her safety, but the trail from the last little park leading up and over the rimrocks led northerly, or behind where Duncan now was. If young Parton made a break for it, Duncan would need someone back on that trail to stop him.

He retraced his steps, coursed the woods until he found Marianne with their horses. He told her what he had found and went with her back along their trail to watch for more of that telltale dust.

They saw it far down the mountainside. Duncan estimated the distance, the time of morning, then, satisfied with both, he led Marianne in a swift passage back to that northerly vantage spot where the trail crossed on out of the park heading along the hillside toward the rim.

He explained what he wanted her to do. She understood but showed him an uneasy expression.

"Sheriff Berryhill will be up here within another hour and a half. You could be putting yourself between two fires, Todd."

He smiled with his lips, but not his eyes. "If this thing isn't settled in an hour and a half," he told her, "then young Parton's a better man than I am, that's all there is to it."

She looked ahead where the grazing horse was meandering outward toward the sunlit center of the park. "You don't even know it is young Parton. It could be another Flying L cowboy."

"Then I'll find that out in the next ten minutes and we can be on our way again."

He faced away from her, already closing her out of his mind and turning his entire attention upon the clearing ahead.

Marianne watched him ease forward for a moment, her face troubled. Finally, instead of going back along the trail as he'd directed her to do, she glided up behind him.

"Todd . . ."

He whirled, his brows drawing darkly down. "I told you to go north and watch that trail," he said sharply.

"All right. I just wanted to say . . . be careful of him."

His frown softened toward her a little. After a quiet moment of gazing steadily at her, he got that little wicked glint in his eyes again and gently wagged his head. "You're still going to get that larruping," he said softly. "Sweet talk isn't going to change my mind, woman."

Her expression altered at once, turning bleak, turning defiant. "Any time you think you can do it, you just try it." She spun about and went swiftly out through the trees northward.

He watched her go as long as she remained visible. He chuckled deep in his throat. *That* was a woman. Concerned and tender one minute, wrathful and fiery the next moment. He let the smile dwindle. She'd said he didn't know what he wanted out of life. He knew what he wanted all right, he just hadn't encountered it before, or at least up to now.

A twig snapped around in front, out in the park. That sharp little sound cleared Duncan's mind in a flash. He swung, dropping down into forest gloom, and raked the clearing. The only visible moving object was that meandering horse. Duncan assumed the animal had inadvertently stepped upon a dead branch. He remained utterly still for a long moment before starting onward again, to the very limit of the last tree fringe. From here he had a perfect view of that creek-side tangle.

The horse was well away from the crushed trail through to the creek. By straining, Duncan could peer as far through that undergrowth as the creek itself. There, where dazzling golden sunlight touched down sharply upon falling water, he saw light reflecting off metal. That, he told himself, would be a carbine leaning in there. But there was no sign of the man who owned that weapon.

It took a little time to get around through the trees to a position where he was close enough to the creek-side undergrowth to pass into it from the forest. After that his course lay defined before him, but it was not an easy one for here he could not advance more than a step at a time. There was no trail, not even a buck run. He therefore had to make very cautious progress in order not to make any noise.

But there was one thing in his favor; all that prickly undergrowth, rank and tangled as it was, stood man-high and it was green so that no limbs cracked or snapped as he gingerly pressed them aside to step ahead toward that unseen place where he'd seen sunlight shining off a gun.

Once his progress was blocked by a chokecherry thicket. Here he tore his shirt getting past, but what annoyed him most was the time consumed working around this mass of twisted, interwoven greenery.

The sun was hot now and that helped. His aches from the earlier fight with Tom Black were lessened by this good heat. In fact, he forgot them entirely as he ultimately came to a little grassy clearing a few feet in diameter, for here he found a trail. This place, from the appearance of crushed grass, was a deer bed, the little pathway leading westerly out of it was obviously the entrance and exit made by whatever animal lived here.

Duncan stepped out into the clearing, shook himself, and carefully straightened up to his full height, attempting to see beyond. On his left lay the little creek and somewhere beyond sight but within hearing was its bubbling source. He passed on over the clearing, started along the trail, and almost at once encountered the little creek. Here he saw tracks where a deer had browsed, drunk, then leaped the creek to wander along through underbrush at the very base of the vertical mountainside. He followed this route briefly, hoping to catch a sighting of that larger clearing farther along where a man's rifle stood. But in the end he was forced to return to the regular little path because of the green wall growing along the creek.

He had no trouble for several hundred feet. The

deer run had been sufficiently used so that the branches and vines on both sides were somewhat broken and chewed off. His advance was swifter now, which pleased him. Also, he thought it very likely that he was quite close to the place where he'd seen that carbine.

He was. In fact he was closer than he thought, for as he gently thrust aside a matting of wilted creepers, out beyond this point there was no more profuse undergrowth at all.

This was the secret place he'd glimpsed from the forest fringe. He carefully eased the creepers back into place, got down flat, pushed his head along with his chin in the dirt, peered ahead, and saw where the creek hurried across this still, golden clearing. He lay for a long time studying the land out there and came to the conclusion that this had once been the home site of an Indian family. The closest large bushes had been stripped of limbs at the lower levels and higher up some branches had been bent into a latticed network for the drying of hides. Rocks had been laboriously brought to this spot to line the creek-bank, containing it so that spring freshets could not make it overflow its normal banks.

There was an up-ended saddle there in the clearing, but there was no sign of the carbine he'd seen earlier. Neither was there any sign of the man who owned that saddle. However, there were things that caught and held Duncan's attention—a clean shirt that had been ripped into strips and lying upon some of those creekbank rocks were several cast-aside strips of cloth that had blood-stains on them, obviously dressings from the wounded shoulder of the murderer he was pursuing.

CHAPTER SEVENTEEN

Duncan's dilemma was simple. He was, he thought, running out of time. Berryhill would find this place before long. Therefore, he could lie there and await young Parton's return from wherever he'd gone, or he could step out into that clearing and locate young Parton's tracks in the spongy earth and go after him.

The latter course greatly increased Duncan's chances of being seen before he got a chance to see Parton first. It only obliquely concerned him, where the missing man now was. There were a dozen logical explanations for his absence and with Marianne and their horses well concealed none of these appeared particularly relevant to Duncan at this time.

Then he heard something or someone coming toward the clearing from southward along the creek. He scarcely breathed while he waited. That unseen moving object halted once where the little creek intersected its pathway, sprang over, and landed down hard. Duncan heard the jangle of spur rowels, and he knew it wasn't a deer then, it was a man.

He felt for Black's six-gun, eased it out carefully, pushed it forward but did not cock it. Out of nowhere a flashing ball of bright blue swooped overhead. Duncan, concentrating on the spot across the clearing where his enemy would appear, had no knowledge of this newcomer, not until, its attention caught by the glittering gun in Duncan's right fist, the blue jay began its shrieking scream of alarm.

At once, across the clearing, all sound ceased. Duncan risked twisting for an upward look. That agitated blue jay was perched in plain sight upon a pine limb, beside itself with excitement. It flicked its tail, bobbed its head up and down in a pointing gesture, and kept up its raucous cries of warning. Duncan, who ordinarily was amused by the antics of these professional, high-country alarmists, wished mightily he could throw a stone at this bird or shoot it. All Duncan did, however, was resume his vigil of the clearing with his back exposed to the overhead view of that squawking bird, and try his best to ignore the creature.

But, whether Duncan's unseen adversary believed the bird's warning outcries involved another man or just a forest animal, he still did not continue forward and emerge into the clearing. He would not anyway, Duncan reasoned. This man was a murderer—a killer—and whether he thought perhaps it was only a cub bear that had upset the blue jay or something else as trivial, his instincts would still hold him back, for young Parton was as shy of exposing himself as a mountain lion would have been in his place.

They both shared the same instincts now. Both were killers and both knew they were hunted as well as hunters.

Sweat ran into Duncan's eyes and some of the scratches he'd gotten in passing this far through brambles began to itch. He was tired and hungry and thirsty, too. His nerves were on edge. He had the feeling of being between two great grinding wheels, one was Berryhill's posse, the other was his compelling necessity to get young Parton alive. He'd almost had Parton, then that feathered interloper had come. Now, he lay there wondering what he must do, for obviously young Parton, with no knowledge that he was also being approached by a downcountry posse, was in no hurry to do anything at all.

Fate made Duncan's decision for him.

While Duncan had been pondering, young Parton had gotten down on the ground to stare along at ground level into the clearing. He evidently had done this with no actual expectation of seeing another man, for no sooner did he catch the wicked reflection of hot sunlight off Duncan's readied six-gun, than he let out a startled grunt that carried easily over where Duncan lay. Parton also shook the overhead brush as he whipped backward, reaching for the Winchester he'd leaned there, when he'd gotten belly-down in the mulch.

Duncan saw that brush quiver. Now he knew

about where Parton was, but he still held his fire because he had no visible target. This was Duncan's first mistake.

Parton hastily poked his carbine through, aimed rapidly at that exposed six-gun, and fired. The explosion of the rifle shot in all the otherwise stillness rattled Duncan nearly as badly as did the stinging dirt that was flung into his face from a near miss.

Above those two secreted men the blue jay gave a frantic leap into the air and went flinging away northward, squawking at the top of its voice.

Duncan, with no worthwhile target, nevertheless squeezed off his first shot, aiming only in a general way toward the place where the underbrush had quivered. Then he immediately rolled sideways deeper into the undergrowth, cocked his gun with his right hand, and dug at his irritated eyes with the left hand. He was temporarily unable to see through the shimmer of water that filled both eyes.

Parton fired again. This time, though, the slug whipped through underbrush with a slashing sound. It obviously had been aimed high in the erroneous belief that Duncan might be up on all fours and retreating.

For several minutes Duncan occupied himself with spitting dust and clearing his vision from the effects of that first shot. But even then his eyes did not return to normal for they were irritated.

When Duncan did not return young Parton's fire, the killer lay silent for a while, but then finally he called out: "Hey over there . . . you hit?"

Duncan considered a blistering answer to this but did not offer it. He said nothing. Instead, he put down his gun, raised both hands to his face, wiped away tears, the last residue of that stinging, flinty earth, and blinked until the fog cleared from his vision.

"How bad you hit . . . you there, across the clearin' . . . you hear me?" Parton called out.

Duncan heard. He considered using a ruse to feint the killer out into the clearing for a good, clean shot. But he scorned this idea. He didn't want Parton any way but in a fair fight.

Finally he called back. "No, I'm not hit, Parton, but you're going to be. You've got about twenty minutes to make up your mind whether to die with a gun in your hand or give up and walk out into the clearing."

Parton's hard laughter sounded. "Twenty minutes is a long time. Why not make it five instead?"

"Because it'll take twenty minutes for Sheriff Berryhill's posse to get up here. He's behind you, Parton, and I'm in front. You don't stand a chance."

For a moment Parton made no reply to this, then, sounding a little puzzled, he said: "Hey . . .

you aren't that stupid Flying L cowboy, are you? I thought you were him. Just who the hell are you anyway?"

"The name's Todd Duncan. I'm the fellow they tossed into jail down in Leesville with your paw. I'm the fellow they thought was riding with Swindin when you killed the expressman . . . and that traveler."

Again there was a long pause. "The hell," breathed the hidden gunman. "I didn't know they'd gotten anyone. Did they get Swindin, too?"

"He's dead, Parton. He was dead when they found him southward at a spring on the desert."

"And my paw?"

"The damned old devil . . . he let 'em think I was you so you'd have a good long head start."

This time the pause was shorter, and Parton laughed. "By golly, sounds like we stirred up a hornet's nest, cowboy," said the murderer, his voice turning almost genial. "Then how come you're out of jail if they locked you up . . . you get loose?"

"Yeah, I got loose, and I've done a heap of hard riding to even things up with you."

"Aw," scoffed the unseen gunman, still sounding slyly genial, "what've you and me got to fight about? I don't even know you, cowboy. Listen, if what you said about a posse comin' up in here is true, and what you said about gettin' loose from the law is also true, then they'll be after you as much as they'll be after me, so why don't we just team up and get the hell out of this lousy country while we still can. That makes sense don't it, Duncan?"

"Yeah it makes sense, Parton, except for one thing. You're going to clear me with that posse for those two murders you committed."

Parton turned silent again. This time, though, the interval of stillness ran on so long Duncan thought Parton might be trying to slip up where he could get a good shot. Duncan's eyes still bothered him but they were no longer watering so much that his vision was impaired. In fact, he could see things more clearly now than before. He turned up onto his side, in this manner presenting the narrowest possible target, and he resumed his motionless vigil with his six-gun concealed from sunlight by hanging leaves.

Parton spoke again, his tone altered a little, sounding not so genial any more, sounding instead a little worried, as though he had digested everything Duncan had told him and had come to some obvious conclusions.

"Duncan? Let's call it quits. There's no advantage in this for either of us. What d'you say?"

"I say no. You toss out your guns and walk out into the clearing."

"You're a fool, Duncan. Berryhill will get you, too."

179

"Maybe, but with you nailed down over there, he'll figure out the truth."

"You won't keep me nailed down, cowboy. I've eaten my share of your kind for breakfast before."

"Yeah? It's going to be a pretty big mouthful this time, Parton. In fact, it's going to choke you. Get some sense, why don't you? Your horse is out where you can't possibly get to him. You're afoot, Parton, and in mountainous country that's the same as being tied to a tree. Toss out the guns and give up while you still can."

"You alone, cowboy?"

Duncan considered his reply to this thoughtfully. He did not believe Parton could get past him to the northward trail where Marianne was hidden. On the other hand, if he said he was not alone and Parton did get past him, he would be on the alert, which would place Marianne in a dangerous position. So he lied to the murderer of Marianne's father.

"Yeah, I'm alone, Parton, but only until Berryhill's men get up here."

"I only got your word there's a posse comin'."

"You can believe it. I cut loose that Flying L rider down in the big meadow and I was one jump ahead of the posse then. In fact, as I rode up out of there, I saw them ride out into the meadow making for that old line shack."

"How many?"

"Six, not counting your paw."

"What the hell . . . I thought you said he was in the Leesville jailhouse?"

"He was, but when I got away Sheriff Berryhill had the old devil with him, taking him to some town named Bradley over in the next county to keep him from getting lynched. The folks in Leesville are really worked up over the killing of that expressman, Parton. I wouldn't bet a plugged dime that when Berryhill takes you back they don't try to lynch you, too."

"Listen Duncan, how much money you want to back off and let me ride out of here?"

"You don't have enough money for that, Parton."

As though he'd been doing all this talking for the purpose of getting Duncan off guard, Parton suddenly fired his Winchester again. The bullet slashed through leaves ten feet south of Duncan, who squeezed off two rapid shots in return, waited a moment, then squeezed off another shot.

There was no more calling back and forth now for a while.

Duncan reloaded, using the bullets from Black's shell belt, tried to catch sight of moving underbrush, pushed deeper into his own hiding place, and let another carbine slug whip through, low to the ground, where he had been but where he no longer was.

Parton switched to a six-gun now. He used an

old frontier tactic. He fired once to the right of where he thought Duncan might be, once to the left, then planted his third shot squarely between those other two. The closest bullet struck solidly into a creek willow several feet from Duncan. He saw the white meat of the tree where bark had been torn away.

For the present Duncan was content to lie still and peer through the foliage. He did not see anything to fire at, so he did not shoot.

Parton called out again. "Get you that time, cowboy?"

"You weren't even close," retorted Duncan. He raised his gun, waited for Parton to speak again, and when the gunman did, Duncan fired three times as swiftly as he could lift and drop the hammer, at the sound of Parton's voice. Those jumbled words broke off in midsentence. Into their wake came a wild threshing across the way. Duncan surmised that he'd either winged his adversary or come so close he'd forced Parton into a wild plunge away. He tracked that wild progress in among the growth, dropped his sights, and fired his fourth round into the middle of the spot where all the frantic activity was taking place.

Suddenly the underbrush stopped jerking. The gunshot echoes diminished downcountry, silence settled. Duncan calmly reloaded again. He thought it possible that he had shot Parton. He also thought it possible that Parton wished him to think this. He waited, his gun resting easy, his body aching from lying so long in one position, his painful eyes rummaging the underbrush across the clearing, feeling very calm and very confident.

"All right!" Parton called huskily. "You win cowboy. I stopped one that time." There was a pause. Duncan listened, skeptical and strongly doubting. "Here . . . I'm goin' to toss out my gun," Parton said.

A Winchester carbine arced up over the brush and landed down in the grass by the little creek. It lay there with sunlight glinting evilly off it.

Duncan said: "Hell, you shot that thing out ten minutes ago. Who you trying to fool, anyway?"

"Here," Parton said, his huskiness beginning to fade as his voice weakened. "Here's my six-gun."

When that weapon also sailed out, Duncan still was not convinced. "You got another six-gun!" he said. "The one you took from that Flying L cowboy."

"It's coming . . . too."

When the third gun fell near the creek, Duncan's skepticism began to atrophy. He flattened, took up a fallen twig, reached far out with it, and shook the underbrush at arms' length on his right. No shattering gunshots came. He dropped the twig, got up onto one knee, pushed his gun cautiously out ahead, and got up into a low crouch. Still no shot came.

Duncan stood fully upright, his chest, shoulders, and head exposed. No gunfire flamed crimson at him from over the clearing. He shouldered through, stepped out into full view, and went ahead as far as the creek and those guns. Here he paused, sprang over the little run of water, thrust a heavy arm into the onward brush, pushed it aside, and looked in.

An unshaven, disheveled man was sitting up there with his back to a spindly creek willow. He looked up into Duncan's face with an expression of hard resignation. "Through the damned leg," he said. "It's bleedin' like a stuck hog. I been leakin' too much blood lately . . . weaker'n a cussed cat."

Young Parton's eyes turned up aimlessly and he toppled over gently, his breath running out in a soft sigh.

Chapter Eighteen

Duncan made a crude tourniquet of Parton's belt, twisted it hard, set it that way until the bleeding stopped. He hoisted the unconscious man so that he was again propped against the creek willow, then left him there.

He hurried back into the forest, northbound. Where the dingy trail passed in and out of dark shadows, he encountered Marianne. She ran to him anxiously, stopped to look swiftly at his body for signs of an injury, then stepped to an old pine and weakly leaned upon it.

"All that shooting," she murmured. "I thought he might have hurt you."

"No," Duncan said. "But Parton stopped one. Not bad . . . in the leg. But he's lost quite a bit of blood from that old shoulder wound, too. Come along. You can help me with him."

They returned to the clearing. Parton had toppled over again and Marianne thought he was dead when she first saw him.

Duncan handed her the injured man's hat. "Fill it with water from the creek," he ordered as he stooped by Parton to ease off his tourniquet. He watched the blood well up sluggishly out of the punctured leg briefly, then closed off the flow again.

When Marianne returned, they worked together

over Parton for several minutes. He eventually revived enough to recognize Duncan. When he set his focusing eyes upon Marianne, they slowly widened. Parton's coarse mouth lifted into a semblance of a grin. He continued to study Marianne but made no effort to speak until Duncan sent Marianne to Parton's saddle out in the clearing for the saddle blanket.

Parton then said: "Little lady, fetch back that bottle you'll find in the saddlebags. I got a need for a long pull on its contents about now."

Duncan eased back on his haunches, pushed back his hat, and hunkered there, considering his captive. "You were a fool not to give up half hour ago," he said quietly.

Parton's pleasant look dwindled as his gaze was now settled on Duncan. "A man's never a fool when he takes the only chance he's got. Too bad you didn't aim a little higher. Then nobody'd lynch me."

"I don't think they'll lynch you anyway, Parton. At least Sheriff Berryhill will do as much to prevent that for you as he did for me."

Parton's lips were gray; his flesh was the same wasted color. He said no more until Marianne returned with the blanket and the bottle. He up-ended the bottle and drank deeply. He smacked his lips as he lowered it with a redness showing in his face now.

Duncan bent over, pulled aside Parton's shirt,

and turned suddenly stiff where he was kneeling as he stared at that wounded shoulder. It was foul-smelling, there was a yellowish exudation visible around the edges of a fresh bandage, and the flesh around the wound for a good five inches was an unnatural green color. Duncan closed the shirt, stood up, gazed into Parton's wasted face briefly. He beckoned Marianne away, leaving the murderer alone with his slack, loose smile and his half-empty whiskey bottle.

"He'll never make it, Marianne. Never in this world. He's got gangrene in that shoulder."

She looked up searchingly. "Perhaps, if he's gotten back . . ."

Duncan was slowly, adamantly wagging his head. "He hasn't the chance of a snowball in hell. You saw that leg wound . . . it was nothing . . . a clean puncture through the muscles. Any healthy man alive would have withstood that and five more like it. Parton's too weak. The poison is spreading through him. He should've gone to a doctor with that injured shoulder ten days back. Now it's too late."

Marianne half turned. She said softly: "I hate him, Todd. I've thought of only one thing since he shot my father. But . . . isn't this going to be a very painful way for him to die?"

"Yes. They don't go out easily from gangrene poisoning. I saw a man die of it once in a cow camp."

She faced back around. "Todd, I don't want to watch it."

"Sure," he said tenderly. "You stay back here by the creek. I'll do what can be done, which isn't very much."

He started away. She spoke his name, her eyes showing anguish. "No, wait. . . . I should . . . he needs a woman there. . . ."

Todd looked at her. "Maybe it would make it a little easier, Marianne. Easier for him." He put out a hand to her. "Come along then. We'll get the rest of that whiskey down him. If his stomach is empty enough that might do the trick."

They went back to young Parton. He smiled up at them with none of his slyness, none of his viciousness showing. He settled his glassy look upon Duncan. "Hell of a way to go out, isn't it?" he said. "Funny how a fellow always thinks it can happen to everyone else . . . never to him. Tell me, Duncan, what's that shoulder look like to you?"

"Bad, Parton. You want a smoke?"

"Yeah. I'd like that. Care for a drink, Duncan . . . or you, ma'am?"

Duncan shook his head and went to work twisting up a cigarette. He lit it, inhaled, removed the quirley from his own mouth, and plugged it between Parton's lips. The dying man inhaled, let smoke drift out his nostrils, and returned his admiring gaze to Marianne. He took a long pull at his whiskey bottle, wiped his mouth, resumed smoking.

Several minutes of quiet were broken when Parton addressed Marianne: "Lady, I know who you are. I made quite a study of Leesville before me and Swindin rode in to bust that express office safe." He paused and removed the cigarette, letting it lie between his fingers in the grass.

"Guess you'd like to shoot me, wouldn't you? Well, I didn't mean to plug your paw, if that's any help to you. I was a mite jumpy. It was my wound made me that way. Your paw raised his arm to point. . . . I fired."

Parton's shoulders rose and fell. He had no more to say on this subject. His gaze dropped away from Marianne's face. He looked straight ahead out along that little trampled pathway where his horse had been browsing some time before.

Duncan, closely watching Parton's face, thought those ruthless gray eyes were turning milky. He stepped up to Marianne, lowered his head, and said very quietly: "Go down the trail. Wait for Berryhill. When he gets up here, bring him to this spot. And, Marianne . . . bring old man Parton, too. I don't think his son's going to last a lot longer."

After Marianne left, Duncan kneeled next to Parton, took the whiskey bottle from the dying man's lap, peered at its dwindling contents, pulled out the cork, and held it to Parton's lips. "Drink," he said. "Drink up. For you, right now, it's the only medicine." Parton drank, nearly choking on the burning sensation of the alcohol. Pushing the bottle back, he lifted a weak hand to dash away the tears forming in his eyes brought on by the rawness of the liquor, then swung his head and tried to bring Duncan into focus.

"Funny . . . since I had to halt here this morning, I've been sucking on that damned bottle . . . and, by gawd, I just simply can't get drunk. That's funny, isn't it, Duncan?"

"Yeah, it's funny. Why the hell didn't you go to a doctor with that shoulder, Parton?"

"It was a bullet wound. Naw. Doctors ask questions . . . they talk to lawmen. Paw tended it for me. He's pretty good at gunshot holes and such like."

"He sure is," Duncan said dryly.

"Duncan?"

"Yeah?"

"If I hadn't turned all weak this morning, I'd have been over those lousy rimrocks by now and you'd never have got me."

"Maybe so, Parton, maybe so."

"But hell . . . when I dragged my saddle off that horse, I knew I was done for. Couldn't even hold the thing. It fell and I fell on top of it. Duncan?"

"Yeah?"

"It's blood-poisonin', isn't it?"

"That's right."

Parton shook his head. "How was it with Swindin . . . did he go out quick?"

"I reckon. When I first saw him, he was leaning there against an old cottonwood tree about like you're leaning now. I thought he was asleep. But . . . he was dead."

"Duncan, I saw the fellow who shot Swindin. Tall cowboy. Shot him square in the back. I'd like to live long enough to stand up facing that one."

Duncan, remembering how Tom Black had looked after their fight, said: "If it makes you feel any better, Parton, that one's had hell beat out of him."

"Good," he said, and closed his eyes for a minute before continuing. "Another thing . . . about my old man . . ."

"He'll be along directly. He's coming with the posse."

"I don't want to see him, Duncan. Will you do that for me . . . keep him away?"

"Yes, but he's still your paw."

"Naw . . . not really. He took me up after Indians killed my folks. I was an orphan and he was an outlaw passin' through. . . . Any more liquor left in the bottle, Duncan?"

Duncan held the bottle up, moved it to Parton's lips, and tilted it until the last drops ran down his chin and the filthy shirt front of the dying man.

He threw the empty bottle off to the left. "Any pain?" he asked.

Parton's eyes swung drowsily. "Naw . . . none worth mentioning. Say, about that girl's old man . . . that was my big mistake, wasn't it? If I hadn't plugged the old gaffer, you wouldn't have been after me so hard, would you?"

"I reckon not."

"I didn't figure on killin' him."

"You said that, Parton."

"All right. To hell with it. Anyway, in a little while I'll be able to tell him face-to-face I didn't mean to hit him." Parton lifted one hand, dragged the back of it across his gray, wet lips, and then let it drop back to his lap as though it weighed a ton. "Tried to make better time over this blasted mountain," he muttered, "but I been awful tired awful quick these past few days."

Duncan heard footfalls in the rearward grass and swung around. Marianne came up and stopped. Around her were a group of hard-faced men with bared carbines. Matt Berryhill was there on one side of Marianne. Jack Thorne was on her opposite side. Behind them, his unkempt old beard flaring out in the light breeze was old Jeremiah Parton, his cheeks hollow with fatigue, his lipless, bloodless mouth pulled back in a grimace, his sunk-set eyes fastened upon the dying man with his back to the creek willow and his tilted, gray, slack face turned toward

Duncan. None of the group moved, having come into view of those two men by the creek willow, and none of them spoke a single word.

"Hey, Duncan, she's sure pretty, isn't she?" young Parton said, his eyes closed, his head shaking from side to side. "But damn . . . she'll hate my guts for killin' her old man, won't she?"

Duncan didn't answer. He just stared back at those expressionless, dust-mantled posse men. His stare was bitter and accusing. Even when he saw Tom Black among them, his face a swollen wreck, he felt fierce resentment for all of them.

"Hey, Duncan . . . you listenin'? You keep that old goat away from me when them posse men get up here, you hear? I don't want to ever look on that damned old devil again. You know how he worked it? He'd send me and Swindin to do the shootin' and he'd stay back in camp, doctorin' his miseries. He knew . . . old Jeremiah knew . . . someday we'd get it. He knew and he didn't figure to be around when it happened. Him and his make-believe preachin'. Duncan, you got no idea what a dirty, schemin', rotten old whelp he is."

"Yeah, I have," Duncan stated so that the men standing behind would hear. "He came within an ace of getting me hanged, Parton. I know all right."

Duncan stood up, stepped away, and made a savage gesture forward at Sheriff Berryhill.

"You want the murderer of your Leesville expressman . . . there he is. I ought to bust you up a little like I did your friend, Tom Black, for being such a stupid, dense damned fool, Berryhill . . . and you, too, Thorne . . . but instead the pair of you get down there by Parton and ask him any questions you might have."

Berryhill looked from Parton to Duncan and back again. He shuffled ahead, got down onto one knee, and hung there, both arms hooked around his carbine, his face solemn and his gaze unmoving. Jack Thorne also stepped up, but he didn't get down. He bent, sniffed the air, rolled his forehead into a corrugated expression, and twisted to look inquiringly up at Duncan.

"Gangrene," hissed Duncan. "Get a good whiff of it Thorne. He'll be dead before sundown."

Duncan stepped away from the three, caught Marianne's arm, and started through the group of posse men, who all stepped aside, looking sheepish. Duncan paused three feet from Tom Black. These two exchanged a battered look.

Duncan said: "Mister, the next time I see you, go for your gun. This is fair warning. I'm going to kill you on sight."

Black's eyes, nearly hidden in swollen, discolored flesh, faltered. "I made a bad mistake," he muttered.

"Yeah, you sure did. The next bad mistake you're going to make is to stay in Leesville. I'm going to settle down there, and, like I said, if I ever lay eyes on you again, Black, I'll kill you."

"I'll be riding on," muttered the vanquished cowboy. "I'm plumb sorry about all this, Duncan."

Duncan pushed roughly past Tom Black, still holding Marianne's arm. He led her back through the underbrush, across the little creek, and out into the large, golden meadow. The farther he walked, the more anger and resentment dissipated in him until, near the north-south main trail, he felt almost normal again. He did not know where she'd tied their horses, so she led him the last few hundred yards, then halted beside their drowsing animals, swung sharply, stood up onto her tiptoes, and kissed Duncan squarely on the lips.

He stopped dead-still, blinking down into her face. For a second she returned his look, then whirled away, untied her horse, and stepped up over leather. Until then, she hadn't spoken a single word to him since fetching back the posse. Now she did.

She said: "Todd, did you mean what you said to Tom Black?"

His face underwent a swift change, turned darkly savage again. He stepped up, yanked his reins loose, thumbed the *cincha*, toed in, and rose up to settle across his saddle.

"Every blessed word of it," he finally snapped

at her, his gaze hot, his voice defiant. "If I ever see him again, I'll . . ."

"No," she interrupted, "I didn't mean that. I meant . . . what you said about settling down in Leesville."

He had to think back a moment to follow out this train of thought for her. His expression softened, though, and he nodded ultimately. "I meant it, yes," he answered. "And there's something else, Marianne. The matter of what I want out of life." He swung his animal over beside her. "Would you care to hear what it is that I want?"

She saw the flash of temper in his gaze, felt the heat of his masculine hunger over that little intervening distance, and reddened as she reined out for the main trail, saying over her shoulder to him: "Well, not right here, Todd. But down in town, after we've both had something to eat and a little time to return to normal, I'd like to have you tell me that."

She went pacing slowly back down the high-country trail. He reined out behind her, agreeing privately. They both had a heap of thinking to do before their lives could resume what had once been their normal, placid existences.

ABOUT THE AUTHOR

Lauran Paine who, under his own name and various pseudonyms has written over a thousand books, was born in Duluth, Minnesota. His family moved to California when he was at a young age and his apprenticeship as a Western writer came about through the years he spent in the livestock trade, rodeos, and even motion pictures where he served as an extra because of his expert horsemanship in several films starring movie cowboy Johnny Mack Brown. In the late 1930s, Paine trapped wild horses in northern Arizona and even, for a time, worked as a professional farrier. Paine came to know the Old West through the eyes of many who had been born in the previous century, and he learned that Western life had been very different from the way it was portrayed on the screen. "I knew men who had killed other men," he later recalled. "But they were the exceptions. Prior to and during the Depression, people were just too busy eking out an existence to indulge in Saturday-night brawls." He served in the U.S. Navy in the Second World War and began writing for Western pulp magazines following his discharge. It is interesting to note that all of his earliest novels (written under his own name and the pseudonym

Mark Carrel) were published in the British market and he soon had as strong a following in that country as in the United States. Paine's Western fiction is characterized by strong plots, authenticity, an apparently effortless ability to construct situation and character, and a preference for building his stories upon a solid foundation of historical fact. ADOBE EMPIRE (1956), one of his best novels, is a fictionalized account of the last twenty years in the life of trader William Bent and, in an off-trail way, has a melancholy, bittersweet texture that is not easily forgotten. In later novels like THE WHITE BIRD (1997) and CACHE CAÑON (1998), he showed that the special magic and power of his stories and characters had only matured along with his basic themes of changing times, changing attitudes, learning from experience, respecting Nature, and the yearning for a simpler, more moderate way of life.